I0521404

"**The Three Priceless Techniques** in Daniel's new book are a transformative treasure indeed, as well as wise, accessible and practical—and I use them myself. I delight in what he has done here with his spiritual parable, a perfect fit for our time, place, and troubled world, and recommend it heartily to all those who seek a better life and world for us all." **--Lama Surya Das,** author of *Awakening the Buddha Within; Tibetan Wisdom for the Western World,* Founder of the Dzogchen Meditation Center.

"This book is an inspiring and delightful tool for daily practices. It teaches simple techniques that today's humanity needs to deal with their day-to-day challenges. It is also a great beginning to understand suffering and connect with your inner Buddha"
--Sri Madhuji

"Daniel, what a phenomenal book! I so enjoyed the story and the teachings. **The Three Priceless Techniques** that you describe (and show how to use in our everyday lives) are so powerful that I am incorporating them into my own practice. What a gift you have written for humanity, as it will change how people look at themselves and the world. You will know you are different and transformed from the minute you wake up in the morning. Thank you, thank you!!!"
--**Dr. Eric Robins**, co-author of *Your Hands Can Heal You*

"Daniel O'Hara brings joy, inspiration and uniqueness to this spiritual journey of wisdom that will touch, heal and uplift the young and old alike. A must read!"
--**Kim Somers Egelsee,** #1 best-selling

author of *Getting Your Life to a 10+*

"Daniel's Buddha Fields is such a relatable story. An investment of an hour will pay dividends for the rest of your life!"
--**Loren Slocum, CEO** of Lobella Int'l and author of *Life Tune-ups: Your Personal Plan to Find Balance, Discover Your Passion, and Step into Greatness*

"Daniel has written an "old soul" book. It's full of ancient wisdom, but it's exceptionally applicable in the modern world. It's evolved, practical and easy-to-use."
--**John Merryman,** co-author of *Your Hands Can Heal You*

"There's a volcano's worth of energy, power, light, and transformation inside this little book!"
--Karen Rauch Carter, author of *Move Your Stuff, Change Your Life* and *Make a Shift, Change Your Life*

"Daniel O'Hara brings practical Buddhism to daily life in his new book, 'Buddha Fields.' In simple parable form, he teaches us how to improve our lives and the lives of those around us without excessive words and practices. Daniel is a master spiritual teacher of the obscured by gently and effectively opening our eyes to the obvious. A great read for anyone and everyone."
--Tom Zender, President Emeritus of Unity

Buddha Fields: Three Techniques to Break Free

Of Dependency for Addictions!

By Daniel O'Hara

Copyright © 2016 by Daniel O'Hara

All rights reserved. Printed in the United States of America. No part of this book may be used or reproduced in any manner whatsoever for commercial gain or profit without prior written permission from Daniel O'Hara. Only the use of short quotations or occasional page copying for personal or group study is allowed without permission.

This book and other titles and videos can be found at:

www.DanielOHara.com

Printed in the U.S.A

Buddha Fields:
Three Techniques to Break Free of
Dependency for Addictions
by

By Daniel O'Hara

This book was inspired by a real person, who was addicted to meth and other drugs, and quickly with minimal challenges, overcame these addictions.

We hope you'll enjoy this most relatable, entertaining story; and more importantly, you'll apply the **Three Priceless Techniques.** They will help you to effortlessly free yourself of limiting beliefs, negative emotional states, addictions, and transform your life!

Whether you have addictions or not, this book is an inspiring story of overcoming challenges and is for everyone.

You can easily read this book in under two hours. Some readers, choose to read it a little bit at a time. Most readers, re-read it many times, as there tends to be an *experience* each time. Many are calling **Buddha Fields** - *The Experience Book.*

Contents

The Crisis

My hand was shaking. My head was pounding. It felt like Mike Tyson was beating on it and with each punch doing even more damage. I've felt this kind of pain before coming off a night of alcohol, drugs and sex; but this pain was more centered around my thoughts and not the toll my body was paying from a night of partying. While earlier today I had a pretty productive day at the office topped off by a nice dinner with my family, none of that mattered now. I was now flooded with the predicament at hand. I was in the hospital and my evening had turned into a nightmare.

I was the *Rep of the Day* as I had set more appointments than anyone else in the office, which won me a bottle of wine. My boss had a kind of risqué sense of humor and liked to buy the brand *Ménage a Trois*® Merlot to get laughs at the office. He, of course, was hot after a couple of the girls.

I made it home through the rush hour traffic and stop and go's. Last week I had to take one of those traffic school tests online for my speeding ticket and learned the definition of *rubbernecking*. It meant your head was going back and forth from the stopping and going of traffic and this expression was true. My neck was sore from *rubbernecking* after just 25 minutes. "Nothing a little partying wouldn't fix," I thought to myself and smiled like a *Cheshire Cat.*

Instead of sharing the *Ménage a Trois* wine after dinner with my family, which consisted of my mom and my sister Linda, I agreed to meet my girlfriends at our local hangout called The Bubble. Dinner was the habitual; my mom made a decent meal and I was lucky in that regard since I rarely had to do the cooking. My mom was cool, but my sister was her usual self. Never ceasing to chime in when there was an opportunity to make me look bad, she would usually ridicule my outfit or my hair. I guess hearing this negative talk after so long, it's no wonder I left the house every night and found refuge in the things that gave me pleasure. Like the traffic, I endured the dinner conversation and was back in my car and off to The Bubble. "I had maybe a drink and half at home, so I was pushing the drinking limit, but I was only going seven miles," I contemplated to myself while weighing the odds of another run in with the *popo.*

Arriving at The Bubble at our agreed upon time of 7:30 PM, was more of a suggestion and less of an agreement. I made it on time, but my friends, as usual, arrived late. While waiting in the car and listening to the radio, I figured since they were late, I should be entitled to the wine I had won.

I always kept a wine opener in my glove compartment along with other *tools* for any type of entertainment or festivity. While I certainly wasn't a Girl Scout, I was always *prepared* for a party. Unwrapping the foil and drilling in the coil like a snake seeking its vein I slithered it in and unscrewed the cork. Pop! I loved that sound! Just hearing it released some of the tension of the day, including the traffic, co-workers and my sister.

I took a few swigs and enjoyed the taste. Or, at least I enjoyed the warmness of the alcohol as it entered my body. I wondered what it would be like to be a famous movie star drinking the really good stuff and if it would affect me the same way. Maybe I wouldn't even drink wine, but sip champagne all the time. Or, as one of the *Real Orange County Housewives* called it *Champs!* When a person is rich, it is easier to call it *Champs* because to the rest of the world - you are a champ! And, when you feel superior, everyone else are just *chumps.*

I could hear Dena's car *The Doppler*. We dubbed it *The Doppler*, because you could hear it before you could see it. It was always making some sort of sound. One day it was the squealing brakes, and another day it would be something under the hood. While we thought we were smart for calling it *The Doppler,* we later found out that The *Doppler Effect* is when you see it before you hear it.

Dena bought *The Doppler* for six hundred bucks and some sex act, which she never completely confessed to. She was clearly ripped off for the $600 let alone having to throw in the sex act as a bonus. Of course, knowing her, she probably thought she was the one getting the bonus! I could never remember the type of car, but it was built circa 1979. While it wasn't a classic car it was certainly a classic *Dena move.*

Dena's car door, like the rest of the car, made noise when she opened it and when she slammed it closed. For the night's festivities Dena brought along another girl, Sandy. Sandy was always negative. If she won five million in the lotto, she'd complain that she didn't win ten million. Sandy had dirty blond hair, a weathered complexion, and a few tats. I didn't know she was coming as that usually meant something was going to go wrong.

As they approached my car door, they saw the wine or, in this case, *our appetizer* before going into The Bubble and quickly snatched it from my hand. While Sandy started complaining about her day, I just ignored her and watched Dena start chugging *my* wine. As she eased the bottle back to its upright position, she paused, wiped her mouth and seemed happy with the taste.

Now Dena started talking about her bad day. I completely missed what she said because all I could think about was her, in slow motion, as she was chugging and savoring my wine. My solar plexus started churning a little as I got out of the car and made our way through the door of The Bubble, our favorite drinking establishment. *Crazy Jack,* who had only one right eye and a patch over the left, hence the name *Crazy Jack,* was the bouncer. He was nice enough to us, since he kind of had a thing for Dena, but we'd seen him get violent quite a few times.

We grabbed three seats at the corner of the bar facing the entrance. This was our favorite spot so we could check out the cute guys coming in the door. Terri, the bartender, put down three drink doilies and said, "What are you girls havin'?"

We didn't think of ourselves as *rich bitches*, as only *rich bitches* drink wine; thus, we asked for three light beers on tap. I noticed that once the frothy heads of the beer were all on the table, we licked our lips in unison. Was it the alcohol, the taste, the raw sensuality of the bubbles, or maybe just the camaraderie of the experience that we longed for?

My eyes and mind quickly moved to the front door. Maybe the girls could see my eyes perking up, so they both turned too. We had our rule, which was to never look at the door at the same time. For some reason, the girls decided to break our rule that night.

In walked two muscular guys. Jim walked in first followed by his buddy, Marco. Marco was slightly tanner and had dark, wavy hair, and appeared to be Jim's muscle. Meanwhile, Jim had a reputation for being able to hook people up with *stuff.* They were both wearing jeans and tight black shirts. Each had muscles that protruded out of their one-size-smaller-than-it-should-have-been shirts. While The Bubble wasn't in the ghetto, it was a biker bar and the clientele was a little *white trailer trash-ish.* Having a little muscle around probably isn't a bad idea when you are in the drug business.

When the two made their entrance, some of the locals seemed to scoot back a little in their chairs and some of them moved forward. From my favorite spot, I could scan the entire bar as if it was like a well-rehearsed orchestra; some moving toward Jim as the conductor and some moving away simultaneously. Dena instinctively turned her head and made eye contact with Jim. The demons inside her were magnetized to the seduction of his wares and moves, and she had a lot of demons.

Jim made a head nod towards the direction of the hall by the bathrooms. We called it *Hook-Up-Hall* because you could get your fix and maybe a little something *extra.* I secretly thought the employees had a hidden camera back there and reviewed it nightly, but I could never confirm it.

Dena was no model, but she could walk a floor. She slithered down to *Hook-Up-Hall.* Jim welcomed her by pulling out a Ziploc bag that contained white powder. My chair position was best for observing the bar overall, but I really had to turn my head to see *Hook-Up-Hall.* From my vantage point, it appeared that she grabbed the bag, and then grabbed Jim's crotch while whispering something in his ear. My guess was she probably told him she'd see him later. She quickly darted into the girl's restroom. As fast as she went in the door, she immediately exited.

Once again, Dena sauntered back to the bar with a smile of a hunter that just captured her prey. It was apparent from the white rings around Dena's nostrils what she did in the bathroom. The question was what did she take?

We grabbed another round of beers. While Sandy was drinking hers, a girl we called *Biker Barbie* approached the bar. Sandy was turning her body away from the bar when *Biker Barbie* purposely knocked into the side Sandy's elbow. This supposed *accident* caused Sandy's beer to spill all over her.

If there was a hierarchy of girls at The Bubble, *Biker Barbie* was the *Queen Bee* of this hive. She had a *Pamela Anderson rides on the back of Harley kind of vibe.* She was about 5'5" with a 38-inch, Double D cup and while she wasn't skinny, her hourglass frame caught every eye in the club; both men and women alike. Sandy, while she'd never admit it, was extremely jealous of her. As the beer spilled onto Sandy's top and jeans, she yelled out, "Bitch!" and it was on! Sandy put the drink down with her left hand and shot a haymaker with her right which slightly glanced *Biker Barbie's* face.

Biker Barbie stepped back to her right, minimizing the blow and wildly attempted to hit Sandy with an open hand palm using her left. Yes, their moves were a little unorthodox, but it was clear they'd both been in fights before. *Barbie* then moved her left hand, grabbed Sandy's hair and followed it up with the right doing the same. Bam! *Barbie* then wrapped one of her legs around Sandy and did some sort of "judo" throw, jolting Sandy's head and body to the ground. *Barbie* was experienced in riding on many bikers' cycles in the past, so wrapping her legs around someone came easy.

The Bubble was a very primal place and since the first utterance of "Bitch!" it was like Junior High School when you heard the word "Fight!" Every head was turned with eyes wide open and jaws dropping to watch the action. *Crazy Jack* was on top of the scene immediately and grabbed *Barbie* off of Sandy. Sandy's head was bleeding from the fall. Terri, the bartender, immediately grabbed ice and began making a cold compress with a dishrag. *Jack* and Terri were a dynamic duo and probably did this procedure a couple times nightly as they moved with efficiency and routine precision.

While Sandy and Barbie were yelling profanities at each other, Jack carried *Barbie* to the door and took her outside. You could hear her yelling at Jack. She held her ground and was protesting that the whole altercation wasn't her fault. While it might not have been, this event was brewing for a while, as wherever Sandy went, trouble surely followed.

Sandy tersely grabbed the homemade ice pack. She proceeded to complain to Terri and express her strong dislike for her assailant, who she now referred to as *Biker Bitch Barbie.* Jealousy was an ugly thing, particularly when the person didn't even know they were so poisoned by it. With all the commotion, I hadn't been watching Dena. Dena's eyes looked droopy with her head moving like a Mexican Yo-Yo twirling around and around.

And then it happened. Dena was about to drop to the floor. While I had some wine earlier and was on my second beer, I still had surprisingly good reflexes and was able to catch her, before she fell completely. The blood vessels in my ears were pumping from the adrenaline rush in my body.

I held her and said "Dena, Dena are you all right?" After about fifteen seconds, though it seemed like minutes, Dena slightly opened her eyes and said, "Daddy, I've been a bad girl." The tone was faint, the speech was slurred to half-speed and I clearly wasn't her daddy. I yelled at Sandy who was still complaining about *Biker Bitch Barbie* to anyone that would listen. I told her to pay the drink tab and that we needed to get out of here. Sandy was still bleeding from her temple. Dena was clearly delirious, and both definitely needed medical help. As I started carrying Dena to the door, I looked around the bar for Marco to find out what the hell he gave her. He, of course, was nowhere to be found. Sandy propped up the ice rag, applied it to her temple with her left hand and helped me with Dena on her right.

Getting Dena in my car was somewhat amusing and challenging. Dena was muttering, non-decipherable jargon that appeared to be mostly directed to her parents. She often complained about them, but these snippets of conversations were surreal. This whole night was surreal. While Sandy and I buckled her in, I saw the wine bottle on the floor and remembered that things went downhill from there.

Once we arrived at the Emergency Room, Sandy again helped me drag Dena inside. Sandy said she was going to the restroom. I immediately had a hunch that she was going to ditch me and the responsibility of helping our friend. While I was still *pretty buzzed,* I was having more introspection on this night than I had normally experienced. I was thinking of events as being surreal, was much more aware of my hunches, and made acute observations of the night's events and details. I would normally discount all these thoughts, so this made for an even more unique evening.

I did my best to fill out paperwork on Dena's behalf. Upon seeing her barely conscious condition, the nurses rushed her back into the recesses of the ER. A few minutes later, a young Filipino nurse led me back to the room where Dena was being examined.

The chair wasn't too comfortable, but I immediately started to recline. I was trying to pay attention to what the doctor and team were saying and doing. I started feeling a little drowsy and out of it myself. The adrenaline was starting to wear off. The intensity of the whole night starting with the traffic, the argument with my sister, the drug and alcohol consumption, and the altercation with Barbie was weighing heavily upon me. However, Dena's condition was the straw that broke the proverbial camel's back.

I was acutely aware of the fact that *I* could be the one lying there, about to die. As I pondered this thought, I asked myself, "Would my friends help me? Was taking alcohol and drugs really worth it? Were my choices a waste of time, energy and money? Was this way of life, my fate? How could I change it? How could I get out of this suffering?" This introspective streak was out of the ordinary for me. I would usually take something to avoid or ease these types of thoughts and emotions.

The Dream

Most nights when I tried to sleep, I would lay there restless; tossing and turning. It usually took quite a while to fall asleep. I often resorted to having a drink or two, or ingesting an over-the-counter sleeping pill for any hope of rapid slumber. I was one of the 48 percent of people in America who suffered from insomnia. I needed something external to help me fall asleep. To break this monotonous routine of lying sleepless, I'd sometimes add one of those plop, plop, fizz, fizz things to a glass of water. It was also supposed to help with sinuses, which also bothered me. I thought, "Why not accomplish both with one dose?"

Watching the white wafer hit the water, the fizz was kind of fun to experience. Even though it didn't knock me out, it was good for a little bit of tension relief. Tonight, for a change, an external substance or bedtime ritual wasn't needed. The stress of the day had fatigued my worn-out body and mind so much that I was quickly asleep.

While, I was still sitting in the reclined hospital chair, I was unaware that I was passed out. I was in such a deep state of sleep, I started to dream. While awake, the world was a reality. However, this dream world seemed to be *realer than reality.* "How could this be more, *realer?*" I thought.

From the darkness, a golden orb of light appeared, moving ever closer into my awareness. Its emergence from total darkness jolted my already *realer* feeling to an even more intensified state. The orb moved closer, and now visible to my inner eyes, morphed into a Golden Buddha.

"Laura," the Buddha said, "The life you wished for when you fell asleep *is possible; it does exist!*"

I was hearing the words of a Buddha speaking to me and it was *realer* than a real conversation. "What in the world?" I thought.

The Buddha continued, "While you think the world you live in is real, it is merely an illusion. It is an illusion of your mind…"

Never having a frame of reference for such an experience, I was wondering what was happening. For a brief moment, I thought I might still be tripping. I'd never had such a vivid and real experience, let alone a dream like this before. I immediately asked, "Why are you here?" Before providing the Buddha an opportunity to respond, I continued and blurted out, "Why are you helping *me?*"

The Buddha, while maintaining his smile and with a grace and tone unlike any other, graciously shared, "Because, you asked." He said he was moved by my desire to get out of misery, and his compassionate nature allowed him to intervene when genuine cries for help warranted it. "Laura, you genuinely have a good heart and I am here to help."

I now paused for a moment, a rarity for me, and took in what he said. As if he was reading my mind, I was wondering what happened to my good heart. He continued:

"The problem is you tend to over-identify the world around you, Laura. You believe your world is real when in fact it is all an *illusion*. You are so caught up in the mode of survival and your own self-inflicted emotions and beliefs - that your good heartedness is rarely expressed or experienced," the Buddha explained and further added, "It is from your heart that happiness, joy and peace flow effortlessly."

In this dream, I sensed something inside me was changing. A less heavy feeling, a lightening of sorts was occurring. For much of my life, I had always felt reactive. When I felt reactive I would grab a drink, take a pill, or find a guy. I thought pushing the limits was exciting! It made me feel alive. I pushed the limits so many times, I was lucky *to be alive.*

This internal feeling of lightness was gaining momentum. While I was dreaming, my physical body not only felt lighter, but so did my emotions. Rather than feeling my standard reactive response, I was feeling an ability to be proactive and to create the reality about which the Buddha was so eloquently speaking. In some indiscernible way, I sensed this was happening or, maybe my view of the illusion was changing? Maybe both? I felt I had a better handle on this whole experience called life. Of course, this whole scene was a dream, and maybe I was just deluding myself. I kind of chuckled for a moment. If I was chuckling during this time of crisis, maybe this whole dream was real after all?

He remained sitting there patiently looking at me, so I decided to ask another question, "How can I change it, the illusion I mean?"

The Buddha smiled and said, "Laura, it is really very easy! I will teach you **Three Priceless Techniques**, and the more you apply these **Techniques** in your daily life, the easier it will become!"

I was dubious, but captivated. I really had the power to change it? And, with only **Three Techniques?** I wanted to hear more. Yet, a part of me was still feeling reluctant to change. Though my life, the way I was leading it, was slowly going to kill me.

The Buddha continued, "Not only will these **Three Priceless Techniques** help you and your life, but these **Techniques** will help others as well. And the more you do them, it will also transform others. It will have a domino effect on the world and the globe will turn into a giant *Buddha Field*."

"Buddha Field? What is a Buddha Field?" I asked.

"Good question," the pleased Buddha replied. "I'll explain that in a moment. But, first in order for you to understand where you are going, we need to review where you have been!"

The Review

With a whoosh and still in my dream state, the Buddha and I were sitting on an imaginary balcony. From this perspective, we looked down where I saw my living room when I was two years old. My parents were arguing, then the front door slammed with my biological dad leaving, which was also the last time I saw him.

Swiftly to the next scene, we were looking at my sister. I was probably seven then and she was pointing her finger at me, telling me I had green hair and green teeth. I was hurt and crying then ran fast into my parent's bedroom only to find my step dad's *Playboy* magazine. I watched my younger self look at the pictures and *little Laura* wished she was beautiful like the girls in the magazine. From my *Buddha Balcony Perspective,* I forgot about this time period and recalled how ugly and unwanted I was made to feel.

Somehow, we morphed time to a couple of years later. I was in the sixth grade. In this part of my life review, I was taken to a moment in time that I had long forgotten. I saw the 12-year-old version of myself, as well as my teenage sisters, staging somewhat of an adolescent tantrum. We pleaded to our mom and stepdad to let us drink. After some cajoling and subtle-threatening, we convinced my mom and step-dad to let us drink. Megan and Mary were 16 and 17 and had lived a lot in those years. My sister Linda was 16 as well and I was 12ish at the time.

My stepdad was okay with the idea. My mother, on the other hand, put up quite a fight. She relented with the five of us ganging up on her. That day, I learned an important lesson - never underestimate the power of a small, determined group to convince others of doing something wrong and dangerous.

After consuming a few beers, my sisters and I were running around like idiots. We made the most of this opportunity to drink. We laughed, spilled, and teased each other. Midway through our intimate beer social, our mother wisely moved the party outside. It was obvious the escapade would come to a screeching halt. What was fun an hour ago, was not so fun anymore. The spilled beer on the ground was the least of our cleanup worries. After having consumed four to six beers each, one-by-one, like teenage girls synching up their monthly cycles, we simultaneously bellied up a cacophony of vomit.

I was the youngest and the smallest. It was only logical that I was the first to project it. I tried to turn away so not to get it on myself, but got it on my leg. To make matters worse, I blew chunks on my sister Linda's new Vans tennis shoes. Her rage was about to explode into a verbal blast. Instead, the only thing she shot out of her mouth was a violent explosion of beer vomit. Megan and Mary quickly followed with their renditions, instead of *praying to the porcelain god* we were *praying to the wooden lawn chairs.* We were hurting so badly it was like we were *prostrating to the chairs...*

My stepdad grabbed a hose and figured while he was hosing down the concrete porch and chairs, he might as well hose us off too. We were four nauseous sad sacks with wicked headaches. Just a half an hour earlier, we were feeling *pretty cool.* Now, we were just a bunch of fools. We all felt pretty-childish. It's a good thing that the laws of the land decreed the legal drinking age 21, as we clearly couldn't handle our alcohol.

As I watched this scene, I saw the sadness and disappointment in my mom's eyes and how concerned she was for me. She had hoped that alcohol wasn't going to be a part of my life. I'm sure she secretly wanted this experiment to lead to such a negative and lasting impression that I would choose to not have alcohol be any part of my life.

I further saw how much my words meant, or in reality how *little* they meant. After that experience, we all promised our parents never to drink again. While observing that scene, I realized the power and importance of words. I had no problem discarding the promise I made that day. As time went by, my words meant so little... like a fleeting fairy tale of white lies, though my life was no fairy tale, it was definitely full of lies. I looked over to the comforting eyes of the ever-present Buddha, who once more didn't move but seemed to acknowledge me processing this experience.

Again, we whooshed to another time in my life, a few years into my teens. My younger self was experiencing a feeling of terror. Fear! Oh wow the fear! I never knew it was so deep within me until I watched this scene. I suddenly realized that a lot of my decisions were based on this emotion. A fear I didn't even know I had. By consuming alcohol, I was trying to numb myself, and suppress my fear-based emotions. I looked over at the

Buddha and while his content demeanor and facial features didn't change, it was as if he nodded acknowledging my introspection.

For a brief moment, I realized I was in a *dream* with a Buddha, while watching myself as a young girl and was able to feel my emotions while watching these scenes. I was even able to think about them. Earlier, I thought my night was surreal, but this was *surreal on steroids*! Wow! I thought drugs altered my perception, but this experience was vastly superior and allowed for layers of experience.

We moved forward in time, maybe six months to a year. Once again, I was deeply moved as I watched myself engulfed in fear. It was late at night and I was in my bed shaking. I could hear the front door open and slam close. My stepdad, like most nights during this time, came home late and was drunk. I was afraid for my mom and that he would hurt her, or worse yet, kill her. Fear! These negative life experiences implanted layers of fear in my psyche.

Approximately one month later, I watched a scene that involved my sister grabbing my arm. I was watching one of my favorite TV shows. She walked into the room and proceeded to squeeze my arm absurdly hard. The pain and unspoken threat, led me to grab the remote control and change it to her desired channel. I trembled with fear and reached out to my mom for help. I called her at work on the phone and started to tell her what was happening. My sister knew I was going to tell on her, so she picked up another phone and got on the call. The phones back then had a cord. Like the phone, I was tethered to my mom and went to her for comfort when I was scared.

I was fearful of what my sister would do to me after that incident. I decided not to ask my mom to intervene. From that moment on, I shifted from reaching out to my mom for help to reaching out for something else. That something else was alcohol. Soon thereafter drugs and boys. As I watched this whole experience from the *Buddha Balcony* with the Buddha's most comforting presence, I was able to gain clarity. I now saw how my life, my choices, my illusions, and my fears shaped my decisions as everything was starting to make sense. I shifted at that moment as if to become a rudderless ship in a stormy sea. I shifted away from my mom and her stable guidance to the unstable foundation of alcohol, drugs and sex. The foundation of my life was based on quicksand and rapidly sinking.

The next scene I witnessed seemed to pause, as if to push down on the hold button. The Buddha, again without changing in any way, gave me time to take this all in. I wasn't buzzed on alcohol or tripping on a drug, but I was certainly in a place of altered consciousness with clearer thinking. I felt as if I was living most of my life drowning underwater, unable to come up for air. But now, I was seeing my life from a vaulted plane; from a pristine mountain top breathing nothing but clear oxygen!

I looked over to the Buddha for guidance and approval. While he didn't reply, I was certain that he knew I understood. Although I was seeking his validation, I felt my spiritual growth on a profound level. I found myself no longer needing his guidance and approval. I knew that he knew we were on the same page. Once again, and, while I was hoping to gain his verbal approval, inwardly, I felt a moment of massive growth as if I didn't need it. Wow, again! I was watching these scenes with the Buddhas presence. This process was allowing me to mature very quickly.

The pause button was replaced by the play button and we rapidly moved to the next part of the movie of my life. This montage brought us to a scene where I saw my teenage hand grab a liquor bottle from our parent's cabinet. I opened the bottle and put it towards my mouth. I felt the ethers wetting my lips and tongue while the alcohol burned going down my throat to my stomach. Shortly after, my pupils dilated with the experience of having imbibed a few mouthfuls of whiskey.

This was a key moment in my life. I often must use the navigation system in my car or on my iPhone, as I tend to get lost easily. I have challenges with directions, so I *drop flags* for locations where I have been. Watching this episode reminded me of dropping a mental flag on this place, as it seemed to be the start of a treacherous route. A route riddled with dangerous obstacles, potholes and hair-pin turns that would play an important role in my life trajectory. As I continued to ponder, I realized this was the moment I gave up my ability to seek healthy, reasonable guidance. Instead, I put myself under the spell and betrayal of a false prophet: alcohol.

For much of this *review* process, I was feeling new levels of elation as I watched these troubled experiences and was feeling shameful. Shame was a drug all on its own. And it certainly wasn't an upper. It was like taking a very strong depressant. Hmm, I just realized that drugs, alcohol and even feelings were all just chemicals. And, all these chemicals altered my blood chemistry. This chemistry either served me, or in most cases debilitated my spirit; driving me to the depths of hell. I was ashamed that I wasted much of my life drowning and never grabbing a life preserver when it was offered.

With a forlorn look on my face and watery eyes, I looked yet again to the Buddha for guidance, wisdom and support. His lips never moved, but, in my head, I heard him say, "You were a teenager, you were so young. You were caught up in the illusion and got trapped there at an early age. Things will be OK!" I was so stuck on the cocktail of *shame and guilt*; it kept me from being able to decipher whether these were his words or actually mine. thunder

We turned our heads to the right and was sent to a new scene. This movie wasn't starring me and that in itself provided some relief. Instead, it was of a circus that was in the final stages of setting up at a new location. We watched a baby elephant being chained to a little stake. The feelings of relief started waning. I began to feel sadness and compassion for the baby elephant. As it was attempting to free itself from the stake, I could then feel its frustration and palpable fear. I paused for a moment and realized that animals are sentient beings, and I was feeling what he was feeling. The scene continued with the elephant trying to break free from his shackle. He tried with all his might and still couldn't.

The scene then advanced, forwarding a year or so, with the elephant still being cuffed to the little stake. As time went on and the elephant was getting bigger and stronger; he started trying less. The scene continued to fast forward another few years, and now the elephant was full grown. He was easily strong enough to break free from his chain and shackle, but he didn't fight it. He mentally resigned himself to being powerless. Sadly, this was based on a false belief that he couldn't set himself free and there was nothing he could do about it.

The scene paused. I realized that from an early age, I developed a false belief system. I believed that I was powerless over my obstacles and allowed myself to be *shackled to a substance, sex, or a person* that would keep me from being free.

The elephant montage was so right on. Understanding now, I suddenly saw my mistakes and was starting to stand a little taller with confidence all while sitting in the imaginary balcony. I realized I had deluded myself just like the elephant. As the elephant grew older, he was physically stronger but allowed himself to become mentally and emotionally weaker. This analogy was also true of me.

It seemed like the pause button was pressed again. I closed my eyes in the dream and started seeing myself in a new and more evolved manner. Not only did I stand taller, I breathed deeper. My shoulders were back instead of hunched over. My eyes were brighter. The muscles, which come to find out there are more of in the face than in the rest of the body, were moving more. My ongoing droopy lips turned into a smile!

I realized what the Buddha meant about my good heart, because I was now feeling it! Rather than numbing myself with *stuff*, the joy that he referenced was bubbling up from within my heart.

The chemical reactions that were happening in my body were better than any that I had consumed. I opened my eyes and looked over to the Buddha, who seemed like he was glowing even more. I realized that it wasn't that he was glowing more, but I was now able to see it more. I was able to see a giant radiating field of rainbow energy that made his appearance almost blinding. Not only did I see it, but I could feel it too. I could feel the Buddhas peace and engulfing love for all. I liked this feeling. "It's like being in Shangri-La," I thought to myself. My increasing levels of self-awareness led me to becoming more and more honest with myself. In that moment, I realized that I had spent most of my life in search of substances that averted my feelings of fear and shame.

We continued to another scene. Prior to the Buddha wisely showing me the baby elephant montage, we watched my teenage-self take matters into her own hands. That scene provided me with a certain clarity that had eluded me until now. My dependency on booze became a way of self-medicating and numbing my growing pains. I used the bottle for temporary relief from fear and other emotions like shame and frustration.

This scene was like one of those *After School Specials* starring Robby Benson. The scene triggered all my senses. I could see a lot of brown furniture and carpet with cottage cheese ceilings. I smelled the lead in the paint, as well as the Black Velvet whisky coming from my breath. I was at

Lance Dillon's home, who lived one block over. We were on his living room couch after school. I was probably in ninth grade around fourteen. I could feel the butterflies in my stomach, which was punctuated by fear. I was trying my best to camouflage these feelings. Minutes later, I lost my virginity on that couch and it hurt more than it was ever described. The experience wasn't at all like my friends made it out to be. I watched how the aura around me diminished. "Whoa!" I thought. Did I just think and internally say the word *aura* around me? I realized that I did and that there was not only an aura around me but an aura around Lance.

Lance's aura, at least for the moment, seemed to grow bigger from the bottom up, as if he was swelling with youthful pride. And, it seemed to have stolen energy from me and was now enveloped by his. The aura of light around his head wasn't as bright. The *halo* above his head, while it was already smaller than the width of his head, shrunk even more. The light that was pouring down on his head began was about the size of the stream from a pitcher of beer. Slowly but surely, the stream started to diminish.

I thought drugs altered my perception! But drugs have nothing on this type of feeling! I was able to see energy now and this new-found world seemed to be even *realer* than the *real* physical world.

The scene advanced yet again to a time when I was fifteen. There was music, alcohol and the air was pungent with the smell of pot. I remembered this night. My elevated emotional state soon fell into a dark pit. Being on the *Buddha Balcony* certainly didn't shield me, or make me immune from experiencing the pain of my youth. It was however, more of a laboratory that granted me the opportunity to develop better chemistry within. This chemistry would result in an awareness of my *Buddha Nature.* However, for this scene I could feel my heart beat faster with adrenaline.

The song *Centerfold* by the J. Geils Band, always reminded of that night.

"My blood runs cold.

My memory has just been sold,

My angel is the centerfold,

Angel is the centerfold"

When I heard that song, a part of me went back to that time and place. I just realized that sometimes my consciousness would shift to eras in my life and I could elevate, or in this case depress my consciousness, depending on the time to which I shifted.

I remembered hearing these lyrics while partying with four boys. I also remembered waking up the next morning to these same song lyrics still playing in my head. My eyes were having a hard time opening. I could feel sticky stuff around them and on my lips. I reached up with my right hand and wiped it away. I looked at my fingers and saw a sticky, whitish-yellow substance on them and smelled it. It smelled like semen. With it still on my fingers, I reflexively reached down to wipe it off on my pants. Instead my fingers touched skin. I quickly realized that my pants weren't on! I was wiping the stickiness off on my naked, right thigh. Like touching a hot stove, my hand jumped higher, again instinctively reaching for my panties and they weren't there either...

I was on the same couch however. I looked around the room. There were red cups on the table, a bong and cans of beer everywhere. My clothes, my top, bra, pants and panties were loosely distributed around the room. I didn't remember what happened, but I will always remember the four boys coming back into the family room and laughing at me. The shame, the fear and the self-loathing was at Mt. Everest proportions within me.

I grabbed my clothes. My blood was running cold. My memory had just been sold and while I wasn't a centerfold, I was the center of their amusement for the night. That night was just like the elephant when he was strong enough to set himself free from the bondage of the stake and stopped trying. I had stopped trying to break free from my imposed shackle. I was in mental and emotional bondage. I was an addict…

The proverbial pause button was sagely applied by the Buddha. My body crumpled up and shrank in my balcony chair. The weight of this experience was heavy, really heavy. Watching that experience reversed all of the above positive, physical traits that my body was so appropriately wearing a few moments earlier. In fact, I was now heavier with stooped shoulders, a very sad grimace, stomach aching with disappointment and the rest of my physical features were one of a depressed person who had lost their way.

Wow, this whole review had been quite a ride. Ups and downs, a couple corkscrews, draining and uplifting at times with an urge to vomit. My body was now heavier in my chair. Physical movement was a little foreign at the moment, since I'd been on this rollercoaster of a dream. At times I was pretty elated, even exalted, but after watching the *Centerfold* scene, I was stomped on and deflated.

The Three Priceless Techniques Dream

I heard someone whisper, "Miss, miss, wake up..." At first, I thought it was the voice of the Buddha, only to realize it wasn't. Slowly with trepidation, I opened my eyes. I was back in the ER. "Oh yeah," I thought, as I was coming to, "I was still in the ER for Dena." The friendly Filipino Nurse said I had fallen asleep and that Dena was going to be okay. Her stomach was being pumped and she'd be ready to go home shortly.

I decided to stand, to further *ground* myself as the nurse brought me a glass of water. The water, while just being tap water tasted really good since I was dehydrated from earlier consumptions. As I tasted the water, I started thinking about the dream I just had. Did it really happen? Did a Buddha really interact with me? Whether he existed or not, the teachings were profound and life-like and sure seemed real.

After waiting for another 40-minutes or so, Dena was ready to go home. Sandy was probably back out on the town, as she ditched us when we entered the hospital. I drove Dena home in silence. We both seemed very different after the night's experience. I thought about sharing the Buddha dream but just before the words got to my tongue, I swerved to miss a cat in the street. Hmm…maybe it wasn't time to share?

I arrived home at about 1:15 AM and after quickly brushing my teeth, removing my makeup and washing my face; I was glad to plop into bed. Exhausted from riding the emotional roller coaster all day, I fell asleep within moments of hitting the pillow.

After only minutes, I heard "Laura, the life you wished for when you were at the hospital IS possible; it does exist!" The Buddha stated, "The world you are living in is an illusion. It is an illusion of your mind…"

The Buddha was sitting there patiently in my dream. While his exterior was one of patience, I could swear he inwardly had quite a bit of excitement in his voice, wanting to teach me more. Maybe this was just my projection, as I was so relieved to see him, and in actuality, I was the one who was excited that he was back!

His presence radiantly showered me with a euphoria of sorts, better than anything I had ever experienced. Far, far better than any drug or substance. It was clear to me that I needed to learn something more to cease the misery I was in. I needed to learn how to calmly control my own mind and emotions, and in turn, how to create these same emotions for those that I was affecting; my mom, my sister, my co-workers and my friends.

While being in the dream and going back and forth between conversing with a Buddha and reviewing my day, the illusion of life began to become clear. It was almost as if everything was a *dream,* or rather as the Buddha said, *an illusion.* I remembered that before we had reviewed my day, I asked the magic question, "How can I get out of suffering?"

The ever-perceptive Buddha smiled and said, "Now I will teach you **Three Priceless Techniques** that with a little discipline, will transform your illusion and thus your suffering." At that moment a full-length mirror appeared on our *Buddha Balcony* and I was now standing in front of it. He compassionately asked me "What do you see?"

I looked at myself and for the first time I really *looked at myself.* I saw the sadness in my face. I saw the wrinkled lines around my eyes. I saw the pock marks on my skin. I saw the emotional scars on my body. I saw the listlessness in my eyes that seemed one step above a ghost. I looked tired, aged and haggard. After this careful review, I turned to him and said, "I'm an addict... I see an addict."

There seemed to be a poetic pause, not for his benefit, but for mine. I realized everything on the *Buddha Balcony* was for my benefit. "**The First Priceless Technique** is to remember that you are a Buddha and that you have a Buddha Nature," he specified with such profoundness.

"I am a Buddha... What does this mean?" I asked.

The Buddha paused for a moment and then said softly, "It means you are awake! You are seeing past the dream, in other words, living outside the world of this illusion," he continued. "When people say a Buddha is enlightened, it means precisely that. He is past the physical form of illusion. He no longer experiences the anguish, misery and suffering like you've experienced in your reviews. A Buddha is filled with *tranquil abiding*, deep peace, and compassion."

He lovingly further explained, "Unfortunately Laura, you are blocking your true Buddha Nature because you are identifying with the world of illusion – the physical world that you currently live in and all the thoughts, emotions and addictions that go along with it. If you break down the word enlightenment, it literally means to *lighten the mind.* You do this by removing your heaviness; your heavy emotions, your negative thoughts, and especially by removing your addictions."

"Wow!" I thought this conversation was like drinking from a fire hose! For a moment, doubt popped into my head that I wouldn't be able to understand these teachings, much less deploy them. I didn't even know what *tranquil abiding* meant. While being filled with deep peace sounded great, it also sounded very unrealistic. I had probably only felt deep peace while on drugs, alcohol, during an orgasm, or in a sexual dream.

I suddenly recognized that when I wasn't thinking, or when my mind was blank, I had more peace. During an orgasm or in an altered state were the few moments where I felt this sensation. I started thinking again… I'm sure a lot smarter when I'm around the Buddha. Or, in reality was I this smart and just dumbed down by the physical company I was keeping? I was again getting so excited to learn how to get out of suffering that I blurted, "How do I change that?"

"It's really quite simple," answered the Buddha. "Close your eyes, put your tongue on your palate, which is the roof of your mouth and imagine that you are a Golden Buddha. Then imagine that a Rainbow Light is emanating in concentric circles all around you. Visualize this colorful light going outward in all directions including above and below you. Continue to imagine the concentric circles of rainbow light flowing outward to infinity while seeing yourself become an ever-expanding Golden Buddha."

Whether my physical lips were actually moving or not, I didn't know. But in the dream, I was smiling from ear to ear as I started applying this technique! As I felt lighter, my stress was rapidly melting away. The stress was now like snow being melted by the light and heat from the rays of the Sun. I was in awe to see how fast this **Technique** was working. I was experiencing deeper levels of peace with each passing moment.

When I took drugs and substances, my perception was altered. In my many *trips*, rather than feel like I was in my body, it felt like I was in a viscous syrup. Explaining a *trip* to someone who hasn't tried it was a little difficult, but the bottom line is this feeling of freedom was better than any high that I had experienced. And, it was free! I would assume it only had positive after-effects, as well. Physically, my shoulders felt like they dropped deep down into the bed. My breathing became deeper and slower, and my face felt like it was glowing. "Wow!" I thought to myself, "This is amazing!"

"Laura, the end result of this **Technique** is to bring about your true nature, your Buddha Nature. Please visualize a Golden Buddha descending from the heavens coming down in through the top of your head. The Buddhists call heaven Tushita." The Buddha paused for a moment as he watched me comprehend and simulate this initial part of his teachings. "As you bring down the Golden Buddha through the top of your head and down through your spine to your heart; you merge the Buddha into you and you into it. From the center of your heart you then visualize the rainbow of concentric circles spiraling outward in all directions. Adding in the Buddha at the beginning is vital to this **Technique's** success because it helps bring about the tranquil and empowering energy from a Buddha to help you cultivate your Buddhahood. This also helps to stimulate your already good heart that we spoke about earlier."

"You can do this technique anytime and anywhere. It is advisable that you do it first thing in the morning, when you wake. You should also do it several times through the day, as you'll eventually start habitually living this way. What is especially important in your case is that as a Buddha, you should never harm anyone or anything. This also means you wouldn't harm yourself. Your body is a temple and thus smoking, drinking, drugs and the like, are items you wouldn't consume," the Buddha powerfully delivered.

He continued, "You are so lucky to have a precious human birth! It is said, the chances of being a human are very rare. The chances are the same as a turtle, on one breath, from the bottom of the ocean swimming to the surface and putting its head in a life-preserver. A human, unlike any animal such as a dog, cat or even highly intelligent creatures like dolphins, simply do not have the consciousness to make the choices to become a Buddha. You are very fortunate to be a human!"

He wisely gave me time to ponder. Normally, I'd be quick to respond or react; however, I just listened. I consciously allowed the depth of his words to touch my soul. Each time he gave me a new example, it was almost like he was sweeping the cobwebs away in my head with a magical broom. I went back in my mind and saw many instances of me hurting myself through my addictions, and how many times I put myself in potentially dangerous situations; that I was truly lucky to be alive. I realized then, that I had been screwing up this life. A *giant red flag* was placed in my mental navigation system. And from this location, great destinations would be explored in the future!

I now took control of the dream and imagined a new mirror in front me. I looked at myself staring back at me. For a couple of seconds, I saw aged physical characteristics and started to judge myself harshly. I only allowed this to last for a couple seconds, because it hurt… I felt pain in my head, tightness in my temples and my breathing was labored. I immediately did as the Buddha suggested and saw myself as a Buddha. "Whew!" I thought as I felt the positive energies coming back into my being. I smiled as I tested myself on this concept and I passed this test.

As I started making the necessary shifts in my consciousness and decisions on how to better myself, I also became better equipped to sense the growing stillness and peace within me and now even around me. The Buddha said it was time for **Priceless Technique Number Two.**

It occurred to me I had already learned the **First Priceless Technique,** and that was exciting. It worked so well and in such a short period of time. I felt a twinge of confidence taking root in me. I knew that I could apply these **Techniques** and that I would truly be able to get out of suffering.

The Buddha asked me, "What do you see when you look at your world? I drew in a deep breath to steady myself. I flashed back to scenes with fights at home with my sister, drinking, drugs, boys, obnoxious people and I said "It is a pretty dark place with a lot of suffering... My world is full of darkness."

Again, the Buddha poetically paused for my benefit. I smiled as I was even more assured that everything in the *Buddha Balcony* was for my benefit. "Laura, since you are a Buddha, you must remember that the location you are in, wherever you are, is a Buddha Field," he said. He paused for a moment. I think he could tell I was getting excited to learn about this Buddha Field thing he talked about earlier. He continued, "The energy that radiates from your Buddha presence, and that emanates from all things, magically transforms the environment around you into a Buddha Field," he clarified. "Seeing past the physical world of illusion, a Buddha Field may have the physical structures; however, these structures are all emanating energy."

He could tell science wasn't my best subject and he slowed his rate of speech to allow me to grasp everything. "The brighter the energy, the bigger the radius and thus the larger the field of influence. In an area or field, the brightness reflects the clarity or advancement and promotes feelings like ease, peace, oneness, compassion and joy. The size of the field and its amplitude depicts the amount of power in its reach and its ability to affect people in a greater distance. Think of it as the wattage in a light bulb. The brighter the bulb the more you can illuminate the dark. In your Buddha Nature, you automatically unconsciously bring love and light to any environment and surrounding," he authoritatively shared.

"Conversely, the opposite is true. The Bubble, for example, is a biker bar and the energy is very dark. Most people that congregate there are also very dark. While there may be a few individuals that have strong energy fields, they use their power for their own interests; their own self-satisfaction with little concern or compassion for others. Being in an environment with dark energy brings out feelings of ego, aggression, loathing, jealousy, anger, rage and fear. These emotions are easily invoked in an individual making them NON Buddha-like. In this state of being, you would easily bring harm to yourself and to those surrounding you."

The Buddha then gave another example. "Laura, people of a similar vibration tend to associate with one another, and tend to live, work and play in places of a similar vibration. For example, people with dark energies associate with people with dark energy. People with light energy, tend to associate with others with light energy. However, people with dark energy will attack people with light energy as they are usually jealous or envious of those with lighter and brighter energy. Ironically, people with light energy, do not tend to associate with people of dark energy creating no disharmony. Looking deeper, Sandy's energy is much darker than *Barbie's* but *Barbie's* energy is very magnetic. Sandy is envious of *Barbie's* energy, and subconsciously, wished she was as magnetic as *Barbie*."

Just learning that I was a Buddha was more than enough to change me deeply, let alone that I could transform my environment and those surrounding me. When the Buddha talked about the energy of people (or aura) and environments, I inherently felt and knew this to be true; however, I'd never heard them spoken of so clearly.

Inquisitively, I closed my eyes and imagined the world around me transforming into a Buddha Field with golden and rainbow, bright light filling my environment. With a smile on my face and feeling an even greater peace, I just realized that peace had levels. I sure loved being around the Buddha as the cobwebs, and gray matter in my brain was now clearing and excitedly firing on all cylinders! My brain felt powerful! My inner chatter slowed. It actually came to a stop, or rather just peacefully silenced.

My inner dialogue was now gone. Gone, as if it never existed at all. However, minutes later, another part of my inner dialogue showed up to fight back. It attempted to fill my head once again with chatter. It tried to say "let's go out, let's go and party!" In an attempt to preserve itself, the dialogue tried to start up again by talking about the lack of talking going on in my head. It was almost humorous. I found this to be so funny. I might have even laughed out loud. I was definitely smiling on the inside, knowing that my inner silence was quelling and conquering my inner demons.

This whole experience reminded me of the saying, how light defeats darkness. I again was in awe of this new depth of thought, and the layers to which I was seeing new realities. Wow!

The Buddhas teachings brought me to such a beautiful place. A place of stillness and a level of love that I had never encountered. It was such a deep state of love, that all I really wanted to do is to share this experience with someone, who would also be on the same level. I was in a total state of bliss! A bliss that I had no frame of reference for. My aura must have been huge!

My drug experiences were nothing like this new-found bliss. My best drug high felt like riding on smooth waves of motor oil and I never wanted to get off. Yes, consuming alcohol and drugs gave me thrills of ups but there was always downs and there was always a toll to pay for the ride. The toll was always financial, physical, emotional and mental filled with disappointments. The natural high from applying the Buddha's **Techniques** was like flying on a cloud; like a ride at the *Happiest Place on Earth.* This high was not of this world, unlike the drugs which were and were only temporary. And sadly, left permanent damage to many of my relationships along the way. I definitely loved this new, empowered *Buddha Me* instead!

With these profound changes I was noticing in my consciousness, mind and emotions, there was a corresponding effect on my physical body. As my mind became clearer in thought and quicker in response, my physical eyes felt brighter and could see with greater acuity. The congestion that was normally present in my sinus passages started clearing up, and the underlying tension in my neck and shoulders started loosening. As my bliss started increasing, my breathing pattern slowed, and the tension in my chest released. It seemed there was a relationship between this release of tension and the decreasing of my heartbeat. This was truly a welcome relief. I always felt like my body was under a constant fight or flight, and now I was feeling free.

I could mentally see a foreshadowing of a future event that a life of drugs, alcohol, and all the other scenarios that go along with it; could be no more. This process was like being in a serene spa where the masseuse would work out the kinks and tightness in my body, melting my tensions away.

I shared with the Buddha that the people in my imaginary Buddha Field were also beginning to glow. I could feel an electrical buzz in the air and it was filled with waves of bright and light energy. My new level of consciousness seemed to enable me to feel deeper levels of peace, stillness and love. The feelings were similar to those I felt radiating from the Buddha, but to a lesser degree.

"Everything in this world is an illusion. In Sanskrit it is called *Maya,* and is based on your perception. Photons, for example, are totally invisible until they strike your retina. Sugar is tasteless until it strikes your tongue. A rose has no fragrance until your nose inhales the pleasant aroma. The sound of a tree falling doesn't exist until your eardrums make it so. These qualities (technically known as qualia) are produced by the mechanism of perception." To further the point, he added, "Most people would think the color of the Sun is orange or yellow. However, the filter of the earth's energy field and your eyes give it the hue of these colors. When seen from space it is actually blinding white light!" With the brilliance of a Buddha, he eloquently discoursed.

I was again outwardly smiling from ear to ear. I was hearing and absorbing his teachings. I was understanding that the world of Maya, or illusion, was an illusion of my own making. In reality, everything was just light and there were different degrees of its brightness. "Very good Laura, you are learning quickly," the Buddha said with confident praise as he saw my physical reply.

"As you experience your Buddha Nature, your true nature, it is very easy to imagine that you are a Buddha. It is very easy to imagine that all that is around you, is in a Buddha Field. Over time and with practice, you won't have to work at this process. It will automatically just be, and you will be in this natural state always," he articulated.

The Buddha poetically paused and chivalrously asked, "Are you ready for **Priceless Technique Number Three?**"

While there wasn't any change in his body movement; I got the feeling by his gentle, yet focused voice, this technique was going to be a bit harder. The first two were pretty easy, so there must be some sort of catch with the third. Maybe I had to put myself into some yogi pretzel position for 24 hours, or fly off to the Himalayas and meet some guru, or give away all my tangible possessions; or maybe, walk around in a G-String voicing Buddha-like quotes! These were the visuals that popped into my head. I wondered what it could be, and with inner exuberance and a slight apprehension, I answered, "Yes!"

"As I said," the Buddha continued, "The first **Two Priceless Techniques** are very easy to apply. The third is also easy; however, most people will find it difficult to apply at first. With practice and discipline, this technique will actually be the most rewarding for you, your loved ones and all others around you as well!"

The Buddha started a new declaration, "I told you before that the world of Maya that you are living in is an illusion, like a dream, a world of your ordinary perceptions. The physical world is an illusion, and the real world is a world of energy. You now have a greater understanding of that reality, from when you turned into a Buddha and experienced a part of your Buddha Nature as Light."

It was at this moment I remembered the age-old adage, "Be careful what you wish for!"

"What do you see when you see others? For example, your mom or Sandy," he asked. I imagined my mom in front me. I weighed her on physically, emotionally and mentally and said, "Well, while she has her challenges, I love her - she is a good person."

"What about Sandy?" he said.

Once I started imagining her and felt stickiness around me, like I was in a cotton candy machine. When I imagined looking at her I felt nauseous and she looked dark. I said, "She is angry and negative all the time and causes a lot of trouble. She is not a very good person."

"When you were annoyed with drivers on the freeway, had challenges at work and with your sister, and were looking for an escape using drugs, alcohol and others; you were emanating from your Non-Buddha Nature. To make matters even worse, the negative perceptions you held of these incidents and people caused you to project negative energies at them. These negative energies actually hurt others. It affects their internal organs, their energy field and further diminished their Buddha Nature.

Along with the damage to them, there was also a rebound effect as it damaged you, as well."

"So," maintained the Buddha, "as we earlier discussed, since you are a Buddha, having a Buddha Nature, you would never consciously harm anyone. This is a Buddhist principle, called *ahimsa* which means non-injury. Applying this principle, you certainly wouldn't hurt anyone with your fists, nor would you hurt anyone with your mind, (your thoughts) or your speech."

He paused for a moment to let this sink in. The depth of his words touched my heart and touched the core of my soul. The Buddha was right. Through my interactions in dive bars, and being in many dangerous situations, I often had to resort to using my fists for self-defense and was ready to throw jabs with my words, and even knockout blows by swearing at people.

"Everywhere you go is a Buddha Field. Remind yourself that even when you don't like or agree with someone, or something; that all people are also Buddhas. The more you judge and see other's negative qualities, the more you condemn them and yourself to the illusion *(Maya)*, causing you even more harm and thus staying in *Samsara,* the world of suffering. When you see the darkness in yourself, others and the illusion *(Maya)*, you are trapped in *Samsara.* *Samsara* is a Buddhist term of rebirth in suffering. You'll keep being reborn in suffering, unless you change your destiny with your Buddha Nature. You are here to uplift others and to see them in their true Buddha Nature. This is **Priceless Technique Number Three.** To remember that others are Buddhas too, and to see them as Buddhas!" he finished.

For the first time in this dream I was a little disenchanted. Though this sounds easy, I felt a great deal of apprehension as to whether I could actually apply this last precious pearl of wisdom that the Buddha had so freely given me. I could feel my consciousness slipping and my confidence waning like a life raft with a gaping hole. My stomach even started gurgling.

With profound wisdom and compassion, the Buddha suggested that I simply give it a try. Trying it sounded easier, though I was committed; I was going to test it. What do I have to lose? The Buddha said, "Imagine you, your mom and your sister Linda sitting at the dinner table and Linda is saying negative comments about you." The simplicity of his words put me at ease. His radiance was something to behold. I reflected that, under these circumstances, my sister would have negative energy coming at me. Perhaps she was just jealous of me? As I watched the scene in my mind, I could literally feel her negative energy coming at me. My ears were becoming warmer, my face felt like it was being hit with hot sand and my gut hurt; almost like I was just hit with a sucker punch.

I was able to feel this *green with envy* energy, as in someone is jealous, specifically my sister Linda. The Buddha stated that the unconscious world of energy was much more real than the physical realm. Recalling these words, it became clearer and I was now understanding how many daily statements were based on energy like *my ears are burning (red);* meaning someone must be talking bad about me, or if a person is *yellow bellied*; they are full of fear or cowardly, and if *someone is feeling blue* it meant they were sad or depressed; all these color references to energy made much more sense.

The Buddha told me to once again imagine myself becoming a Buddha of pure light and love, and then to see the dining room and my house as a Buddha Field of golden and rainbow, radiant energy. The Buddha told me to re-imagine my sister and mom turning into Buddhas of pure light and love as well, by applying **Priceless Technique Number Three.** With much apprehension, I followed the steps, and to my amazement, I felt an incredible sense of lightness and bliss taking me even higher than I had felt earlier in the dream. Wow, the Buddha was right! The **Third Technique** was the crown jewel of the three.

In this moment of reflection, I realized the profound similarity of being and seeing people as pure light and love, and remembered that the word enlightenment meant being light, or not entangled with grosser, heavier energy. "Light felt good," I thought. This was better than any drug I had tried.

My lips seemingly moved on their own accord as I started smiling. I never realized until now, just how much stress I had previously carried in my facial muscles. It seemed as though when I became *lighter and full of love,* it was easier to feel free, be full of energy and experience a *natural high.*

"How many people know about these **Three Priceless Techniques?**" I asked.

"Not enough…" the Buddha wittily replied.

Who would have thought that the Buddha, along with his omniscience, also possessed humor, timing and wit? I thought it might have been my imagination, but I could almost feel a sense of sadness emanating from the Buddha. I realized it wasn't sadness, but rather compassion. I could feel his compassion of wanting to spread these **Techniques** for all to experience, while simultaneously felt his sadness that people were ignorantly hurting each other with their interactions. This realization gave me a boost of energy - a confidence and purposeful feeling as if I was part of something bigger.

"Well," I said, "how many people would be enough?"

"Great question!" the Buddha fired back a reply. "There are approximately seven billion people in the physical world on the earth. If seven million or more could do these **Three Priceless Techniques** consistently at the same time it would create a wave of energy, literally a positive tsunami of energy, which could transform their physical world into a Buddha Field...forever."

The Buddha further explained when a person becomes a Buddha, their energy field expands more than ten times. As they create a Buddha Field, the frequency of that location is also expanded and multiplied by yet another ten plus times. When you see others as Buddhas, again their expansion is increased another ten times. And as other people do it together at the same location, the energy is multiplied by still another ten-fold. He alluded to speaking more about group application of these **Techniques** at another time and how it dramatically multiplied everything.

"So, you see Laura, the Earth needs at least seven million people doing these priceless **Techniques** simultaneously and repeatedly," the Buddha concluded.

I mentally did the math. 7,000,000 people multiplying their energy 10 times, the energy of the location 10 times and simultaneously multiplying the energy of others by 10; that might just equal seven hundred million people, or roughly 1/10th of 1% of the population. The wave of Buddha Fields from this number of people could be enough to help all seven billion people. The Buddha seemed to be smiling even more as he saw I was on to something. I thought it was pretty cool I could do math in a dream! Now…work to be done!

Coming Down

Boom! I landed in my body. Actually, it felt like I crashed into my body. The alarm was screeching... The shrill sounds that come with alarms are enough to drive a person to drink. "Why couldn't the clock manufacturers do a deal with U2 and buy the rights to play *A Beautiful Day* upon waking?" I briefly thought. I surmised that the drug companies probably paid the clock guys more money, because if everybody was happy and singing songs; there would be no customers for their drugs.

The Buddha dream world was over, and the heaviness of the physical world was once again upon me. As the weight of my hand hit the alarm clock, it seemed lighter than usual. I collected myself as I showered. My negative internal dialogue started to try to call the dream into question and tried to deny the dream's existence. My newfound countenance quickly shrugged it off. It also seemed as if the world of dreams and the *real* world were merging.

With the highest mental and emotional clarity that I had ever experienced, I recounted **The**

Three Priceless Techniques, "Become a Buddha, transform the surrounding area into a Buddha Field, and most importantly, visualize everyone in that Buddha Field as a Buddha of pure light."

In the shower, I imagined myself as a Buddha and felt the anticipated stress of the day begin to melt away just like it had happened in my dream. I could feel my sinuses clearing, my shoulders relaxing and my blood pressure dropping. These physical responses were confirmation that the **Techniques** were working and that my dream is reality.

I was the first one out of the house and didn't get a chance to *Buddha-ize* my family. I quickly grabbed a cup of coffee. I had such a spring in my step, that I spilled some on my pants. Normally this would have set me off, but I was handling things in a pretty chill manner.

Typically, the *rubbernecking* would also really irritate me, but as I drove down the familiar 405 Highway, I visualized the bumper-to-bumper traffic as a Buddha Field of multi-colored, metallic lotus flowers each carrying Buddhas. I really liked this creative visualization, and thought the Buddha would be proud of my improvisation. As two drivers cut me off, the old me, the *Non-Buddha Laura* would have referred to them as idiots and I probably would have given them *the bird.* Instead, I mentally blessed them by seeing them as Buddhas with greater awareness and consideration towards their fellow drivers. Each time I did this, I noticed my demeanor becoming even more calm, peaceful and serene, and as if by magic, the cutting off of cars stopped. Normally each negative event would worsen my mood, escalate my negative emotions and elevate the pressure around my temples. Now each negative experience reinforced an even more positive energy. These **Techniques** were truly transformative as each negative interaction made me feel even better! The rest of the drive flowed with ease as I arrived at the office parking lot. Instead of feeling drained, I felt invigorated!

Sally, the receptionist, was engaged in multiple conversations and looked stressed. I immediately saw the office as a Buddha Field, and saw her transforming into a Buddha of luminous light. As I walked past her, I thought I could feel her field of energy changing. If I wasn't mistaken, it appeared to grow larger and gently merge through mine. Our collective energies were merging, and we were transforming the environment together.

This interaction planted seeds within my consciousness for later exploration.

As I pulled out the chair to my cubicle, I heard her tone change and could hear that she was surely smiling as she warmly greeted new callers and effortlessly helped re-connect those on hold. "So far so good," I thought. "This was easy."

I put my coffee down and got my desk organized for the day and turned on my monitor. There was an email waiting for me from my boss, Will Frank. Will, like many of the CEO's today was younger and in his late 30's. He was an okay guy. He mostly told me the truth, but many times would leave me hanging when it came to getting paid. While I never told him how much it pissed me off when he made up some sort of excuse why my check wasn't ready, I pushed these emotions inside me.

Will's email asked me to come see him when I got in. I got up and proceeded down the hall. I could hear Sally smiling as she was speaking with people and it made my heart smile and feel good.

The door was open and with two of my knuckles I rapped on the door to make myself known. Will was on the phone with whom I guessed was his wife. They were having marital problems, and he was spending a lot of time on the phone with her lately. He motioned for me to come in and sit down. He told his wife he had to go and clicked off his iPhone.

He said he wanted to work on selling a new product. He wanted me to set appointments for people that were in foreclosures and let them know how we could save their homes. He started painting this grand picture of how noble it would be and *blah, blah, blah.* Nobility and Will were only connected if there was going to be a profit for Will. In spite of my lifestyle, I took my job seriously and was an excellent appointment setter. Not many people could handle the rejection, the violent hanging up of the phone, the yelling and the overflowing of condescending people. Spending a day on the phone was like running a gauntlet with people trying to prod and poke me with red hot steers.

I wasn't too excited about this as I was in a groove with our current promotional program, and liked winning on an average of two or three bottles of wine a week. But, he was the boss. He gave me my script and the list I was to call and had IT load my computer with a new list. I was to be calling a suburb of Detroit. Detroit was in dire straits as the car manufacturers moved to places like Tennessee and Mexico.

My dialing machine was turned on, and the action began. The machine would dial four people at the same time and connect me with the one who answered first. A lady answered, and I asked for George White. And, damn it hit me. It felt like my gut was punched by an uppercut. Before she even answered with "Who's calling?" I could feel her fear! I could feel the fear of her families' survival and their despair. Oh my, this hit me to the core. I flashed back to my montages and remembered scenes where I had fear.

My *Buddha **Techniques*** went out the door. I felt like Laura again and I didn't like it. I made a few phone calls, and in my mind, I was praying that no one would answer, so I could go on my cigarette break. My dialer made another forty-three calls and I spoke with six people; three violent hang ups, two no interests and one call back after 5PM. I quickly grabbed my purse and my trusty cigs.

I went outside of the building and quickly lit one up. There were two of my co-workers standing by the bushes doing the same. They were doing the usual; complaining about their boyfriends, our boss and some of the people they spoke with on the phone. A few people walked by and gave us stares as they probably didn't like the smoke.

While I thought about this in the beginning, much like my cold-calling job, I was immune to others and how they saw me smoking. This was the first time, since when I first started smoking that I even thought about how other people reacted to my puffing away. Instead, I liked concentrating on the inhalation of the smoke going up and down in my throat and lungs and feeling my breathing pattern. I flashed to the dream of me in a G-String as a Yogini and thought, "hmm…maybe there is a connection between yoga breathing and smoking and this whole awareness of breathing thing."

My introspection was broken up by the glare from a man in a well-dressed suit, who was intently looking down on the three of us. I surmised it was because we were smoking and filling his pathway with a smoky cloud. I could feel his ire blasting me with his thoughts. It seemed that this day was filled with a sensory overload. An overloading of all my senses – especially feeling others and the energy of each situation.

To protect myself, I took several deeper drags on my Marlboro and tried not to think, feel, or analyze like I had been doing for the past twelve hours.

I went back inside, turned myself on autopilot, put my head down and started making more calls. My phone beeped with a text from Dena wanting to go out tonight. Given the night she had last night, she was in no shape to go out again tonight.

What was I to do this evening on my own? Breaking out of my robotic state, I thought of the quote, "Idle hands are the Devil's playground..."

In the car and since this morning, I hadn't thought too much about the Buddha dream. Did it really happen? Was I really a Buddha? Was I even ready to become a Buddhist? Was that even a requirement? I momentarily chuckled, which was probably the first time all day. I don't remember the Buddha even mentioning whether I had to become Buddhist or not. I visualized myself with a shaved head and a robe. I laughed again. I laughed a little more that while I often shaved down below, my walking around bald on top wouldn't attract the attention I liked!

I felt like having a drink, or maybe even some harder *stuff.* Since the Buddha wasn't around, I figured I'd find some company. Besides, misery loves company. I thought I'd try to eat a little *healthier* tonight and go to Subway to Eat Fresh and then hit up an AA meeting.

I grabbed a chicken sandwich and felt good about all the produce going into my Oat Bran foot long. Normally, I would have ordered White Bread along with a Large Coke. But I was determined to *eat healthy,* so Oat Bread and a Small Diet Coke was on my order. Maybe I was making some progress after all and was at least, harming myself less... I dined by myself and saw families and singles coming in and out. Most of the families had kids in soccer uniforms and were excited to order their sandwiches. Some kids liked everything while others were very particular and just wanted meat, cheese and mayo with no produce.

I finished my meal and the people watching entertainment, and was on my way to the meeting. Arriving at the parking lot, there were several people outside chatting it up and smoking cigarettes. It was clear that this gaggle of people, myself included, would just replace one addictive tendency for another.

Addiction was like a game of *Chutes and Ladders.* Sometimes you were going up, meaning you replaced an addiction with a *less negative* one like stopping cocaine to only do pot, or pot to only smoke cigarettes. You might have a few good rolls of the dice if you moved from meth to Marlboro's, but one wrong roll and you were back on the horse, often while riding some biker named Hank who was hopefully hung like a horse; all in one night.

The meeting was ready to start, and we were all sitting around in a circle. The circle was supposed to make everyone equal in stature, but while well intended, this usually wasn't the case. There were people of all walks of life in the group. Most had other addictions on top of alcohol. An exec with a coke habit, a young girl addicted to sex, an African American girl who, judging by the tracks on her arms, was into some pretty hard stuff. I had seen people who had the same amount of needle-marks on their arms and unfortunately, they didn't make it. There were also several *Joe Six Packs* who probably worked as brick layers, or some blue collar trade, that were *just alcoholics.*

There was a new person named Larry and while he looked like he had his act together, he clearly did not. He explained how he'd wear a suit and tie, or at a minimum a vest to make himself look better to the outside world. But, on the inside, he had a deep dark ugly secret and would sneak it in whenever he could. His drink of choice was odorless vodka, and when vodka wasn't around he'd drink mouthwash just for the taste and feel of the alcohol.

Larry affirmed to the group that "I am an alcoholic…" I made a mental note and *planted a memory flag* in my *mapquest-like brain*, as when Larry said that, for the first time I questioned the use of the term, "I am an alcoholic." In fact, my body kind of shuddered and I felt congested after he uttered those words. Larry saying these words didn't seem to be completely true. This is the first time I had this revelation which wasn't quite clear. I questioned, Larry drinks alcohol excessively which would normally add up to addiction so thus he must be an alcoholic. Right?

I reflexively remembered back to simple math; if A = B and B = C then A = C which meant Larry is *an alcoholic!* As I said those words in my mind, automatically labeling and condemning Larry, it just didn't feel good or right. Suddenly, the guy next to me changed his sitting position and as he crossed his leg, the toe of his boot hit me just below my knee. This perturbed me as I was just starting to get into some pretty deep *Buddha-stuff* but the physical world reared its ugly head.

I watched the group and leader talk about their own issues and further thought to myself, that while we're sitting in a circle, this circle was a metaphor for this type of group. They were just going around and round in a circle and still stuck in an illusion. It was kind of like the *Samsara* thing that the Buddha mentioned.

The room was well lit but was kind of dark from an energetic perspective. The participants certainly didn't glow. Most of them had dark bags under their eyes, and deep ceded lines above their lips from the puffing of a cig motion they've clearly been making since their early teens. The deep wrinkles always reminded me of people being weathered from working hard in sun drenched crops all their lives. They all sat with a side slump and looked as if they were struggling to stay awake. The room felt heavy and the air actually felt sticky and balmy.

I left the meeting in a hurry and tried not to speak to anyone on the way out. What would I say? I remembered the scene from the Buddha telling me about the darkness around The Bubble. He said that people tended to gravitate towards people and places that matched their own energy or aura. While I didn't know what my aura looked like, I hoped it didn't mirror any of these people and started to feel like I didn't belong in this place or this group.

I got home and like after the AA meeting, I tried to avoid running into my family for any type of small talk. I sneakily went to the fridge for a beer, and went to the bathroom to search for the *plop, plop, fizz, fizz* to help me get some sleep. I had a tough, tough day and was truly tired of feeling and thinking and just really needed to get some sleep. If I didn't get to sleep soon, I'd probably make a run to The Bubble.

It was 11:15 PM and I was wide awake after 30-minutes of tossing and turning. Still so wired after the day, I got out of bed, grabbed my pants and shirt, no bra and headed for The Bubble. A drink or two would calm me down and maybe I'd hook up with Mike, or as I liked to call him *The Bear.* He was an IT guy with a beard and a belly. I kind of liked his belly because it didn't make me feel self-conscious about mine.

My consciousness and my car were both on auto-pilot mode recognizing all the curves and turns to The Bubble without me having to do much mental work. Life would be simpler if I didn't have to think, and especially feel. I didn't like to feel...

I grabbed a seat at the bar. Terri, before asking "what are you havin'?" asked how Dena was doing. I told her about her stomach being pumped and our late night at the hospital. She grabbed a Lite Beer on draft, set it in front of me, and said "It's on the house!"

I threw a few back in about 30-minutes time and enjoyed the feeling of the alcohol in my bloodstream. This was a feeling that I enjoyed. It had been about 24 hours since my last taste of alcohol and I missed it. It was also the first time I was able to "relax" all day.

Several years ago there was a church around the corner. When I would ride my motorcycle nearby on Sunday's, I'd see bumper stickers with W.W.J.D. It, of course meant, "What Would Jesus Do?" This question prompted me to think, what would the Buddha think of me right now?

This thought hit me hard. I sunk in my chair I felt shame and sadness, and that I had disappointed him.

I then felt a slap on the back of my head. It didn't feel Buddha-like. I cautiously, yet quickly turned my head and tried to turn my body to create space. It was *Biker Barbie* asking me where *Dena the Douche* was. I said she is over there and pointed towards *Hook-up-Hall.*

Barbie took the bait and turned her head looking towards the hall. As she did, I swung an open slap to her left temple and landed it! She wobbled, caught herself and came at me full force swinging both her hands. She connected with a couple shots to my face and grabbed my hair. While I was looking for physical action tonight from *The Bear* I wasn't looking for a *bear hug* from *Barbie.* With her hands grabbing my hair, she kneed me in the solar plexus which put me completely to the ground.

The next thing I knew *Crazy Jack* was helping me up. I asked him how long was I out for? He said not long and helped hobble me up onto my stool. *Barbie* was nowhere to be found. My guess was she was escorted out, just like last night. After a few minutes of collecting my wits, I asked Jack to escort me to my car. I figured I was now fatigued enough to get some sleep.

My car seemed to know how to get to The Bubble better than knowing how to get me home. My mind must have still been foggy after the squabble, as I had to think extra hard to drive the route back home.

Finally, tip-toeing into the house and making it back to my bed, I dropped down, clothes still on and was out like a light.

The Review of the Day

My eyes were heavily shut, but it seemed as if my eyelids were becoming thinner and transparent as there was a bright light in the distance. A golden light seemed to be coming steadily at me. It first started small and far away, then closer and familiar. I could now distinguish the outline and shadow. It was the Buddha! I thought for sure he'd be frowning at me, and was about to give me a lecture. Instead, he just floated above me, smiling and was his beautiful, golden, radiant self. I already felt calmer in his presence. My thoughts slowed, my fear meter dropped, and my shame was subsiding.

The Buddha asked, "How was your day?" I thought, I had once experienced the Buddha having humor and perfect timing, but this made me laugh, because I knew he already knew how shitty of a day I had. But it felt good to laugh. There was no denying it. Everything the Buddha did, said, and didn't say made me feel good. If there was a drug called *Buddha-uana*, I would be smoking it every day! I again laughed and remembered that as a Buddha, smoking was a no-no...

He said the day was a wonderful day for me. "Wonderful?" I said. Maybe, he didn't see the turn of events of my day? Then I realized what he meant. Today was wonderful *because* of the events. The drama and illusions of *Maya and Samsara* were attempts and tests for me to apply the **Three Priceless Techniques** I had learned. Disappointedly thinking back on my day, I had many chances to apply them; but I failed. "F.A.I.L. simply means 'First Attempt in Learning' and I was definitely successful at that," he said.

We reviewed the day's events. In essence, I had been doing great up until I left Will's office and started getting caught up in the dramas and traumas of my emotions and in the emotions of others. The Buddha acknowledged, "You showed a higher level of spiritual maturity. You had compassion for others, and you were sensitive enough to feel what they were feeling. Your heart was awakening your compassion within."

He further went on to say, "That instead of wallowing in their misery and joining in their suffering realm, it would have been better to apply **Priceless Technique Number Two**." Suffering in the illusion *(Maya)* is what the Buddhist's call *Samsara,* he again reminded me. *Samsara* was certainly where I was with my consciousness, I mentally acknowledged.

The Buddha continued stating, "The difference between *Samsara* and *Nirvana,* is that *Nirvana* is the realm outside of suffering, and is reached by continually practicing the **Three Priceless Techniques** and more, which help to elevate your consciousness to this vaulted plane." My thoughts reverted to my high school biology class. Most people were like the frogs in a pot that was gradually brought to a boil; stuck and unable to get out. The start of the boiling water, just like the first drink of alcohol or puff on a cig, soon leads to a cauldron of bubbling, boiling water. Thus, causing them to swim in circles; miserable, stuck, and unable to go anywhere because they didn't have the knowledge to make the necessary adjustments to the temperature change. Without knowing the **Three Priceless Techniques,** a person could boil, in essence, boil themselves to death. This visual reminded me of the Catholic's version of *burning in hell.*

The Buddha could see what I was thinking and said I was correct; addictive tendencies drove people to what the Buddhist's called the *Hungry Ghost* realm. Meaning, a person would try to satisfy themselves with alcohol or drugs over and over again, only to be stuck in the same dark pattern. In this realm, they're unable to consume enough through their small starving mouths, causing them to keep searching for more; looking endlessly for the next best thing thus called *a hungry ghost.* The Buddha said I should have instead seen my friends and acquaintances as Buddhas to help accelerate theirs and my eventual trip to *Nirvana.*

Wow! This was deep stuff. The Buddha wisely paused. I started thinking about a couple I knew that ironically were named *Sam and Sara* and they fought all the time. I used this as a memory tool to remember this concept of *Samsara.* His last explanation reminded me of a sales trainer that came to our office last year and started his talk by asking the question, "What is the best thing you can do for poor people?" After a pause, he answered his query with, "Not be one of them!" The room of course laughed. This whole *Samsara* and *Nirvana* explanation wasn't a laughing matter - it was serious! "The best thing you could do for people in *Samsara* was not be one of them," I thought.

The Buddha saw that I was done with my interlude of processing his wisdom and moved on.

We montaged to the AA scene. He also complimented me on understanding that someone identifying themselves as an alcoholic, was not good. He said, "Yes, awareness is the first step to change and while AA provides a lot of benefits for people, such as acknowledging that they have a problem and providing a support group with accountability; the labeling of themselves as their problem was shackling themselves to *Samsara*. They would have been better off acknowledging that they were a Buddha; someone who is awake, outside the prison of *Samsara,* and more importantly, someone who would not injure others or themselves. One of best things that AA addresses is character building! We'll come back to that later."

His elaboration made sense. During the AA Meeting, I was trying to figure this whole thing out. Fortunately for me, his cogent communication, as usual, made it crystal clear. The Buddha gave me two compliments and showed me the scene of me smoking. He just sat there smiling. "Ouch..." He was right. I was smoking today which was very un-Buddha-like. I felt bad that he was spending all of his time teaching me, and felt like he had better things to do, or others that needed more help. Gosh, I had better get my act together. His time and humble wisdom provided me with another bit of encouragement.

He said I was on the right path regarding my connection of smoking and breathing. And, that smokers, while on one level were using smoking to numb themselves from pain; they were, however, unconsciously connecting to their breath. They would have been better off doing breathing exercises instead. He said we'd come back to that subject in the future. I immediately smiled! Knowing the Buddha would always keep his word this statement just meant I'd get to see him again and there was more to learn!

He showed me a scene where I went back to The Bubble. Before he even started the review, I put the **First Priceless Technique** into action and was already starting to get the answers! This was exciting knowing that I could just visualize myself as a Buddha which helped put me in the right frame of mind. Tapping into this enlightened perspective, as in, knowing everything, I knew that I never should have been at The Bubble in the first place. When I was lying in bed with so much frenetic energy, I should have put on my *Buddha-Suit* and become a Buddha. By doing so, I would have calmed down, silenced my addictions and had a most blissful night of slumber. Possibly even hanging out with other Buddhas in my dreams. "Oh wow, there are other Buddhas?" *I epiphonized!*

The Buddha, without changing his facial expression, was pleased with my newest realization that there may be more than one Buddha! I could have sworn I heard him say, "We'll talk more about that later!" My own mental lesson continued with me as the Buddha. My *Buddha-self* realized that if I was to ever be in a fight, I should do everything I could to try to see that person as a Buddha. And, if this didn't work, just because the other person was suffering didn't mean I had to suffer too, and that it was okay to defend myself.

I had a cousin who was a police officer named Peter. My sister and I called him *Peter Popo.* Peter talked about using excessive force on people all the time. However, cops were only supposed to use the minimal physical force necessary to apprehend a subject. It seemed from a Buddhist perspective, my guess would be to see others as a Buddha, avoid the fight if possible and then defend yourself... and try to defend with only enough force necessary to get out of the confrontation.

"Whoa! I had learned a lot on this review."
I saw how events during my day triggered me to not
only stay in *Samsara,* but depress myself into
deeper levels. Hmm, maybe *Samsara* was like the
hells in the Bible and that there were levels. Wow,
I was learning so much! Just then, our cat jumped
up into my bed and woke me up.

"Damn cat!" I thought, and realized I was
just yelling in my mind at a cat for abruptly taking
me away from dreamtime with the Buddha. I was
damning our cat knowing that a Buddha wouldn't
do that. A cat was just a cat, right? He wasn't
enlightened, I quipped. I just realized the word
spelling was actually *spell-ing* as in our words are
like spells. I saw myself as a Buddha; I saw my
room as a Buddha Field and saw the cat as a
Buddha. I felt fantastic! I was quickly out again,
having the best night of sleep in my adult life and
even thought I remembered the Buddha saying,
"We'll talk about animals and how you can help
them in the future!"

A New Day

Ahh... It was as if a feather dropped from heaven, moving wispily back and forth in the wind, which was the best way to describe the way I landed in my body that morning. My alarm went off with its claxon sound announcing a new day. Normally, when I woke up, my body felt so heavy, but this morning I moved with a new lightness.

It was as if the day welcomed me into her bosom and was nurturing my being, with a new zest for life. My normal *Laura-self* tried to start talking about all these new feelings and tried to sway me away with "How about an Irish Coffee or a Bloody Mary to start off the day?"

I remembered a judo class I took at the local Community Center when I was a kid, that I was to welcome hit the attacker, merge with the attack and re-direct the force. I put on my *Buddha-Suit* and allowed the thoughts to come. I merged the thoughts into my Buddha Nature and soon they were re-directed away. Having this feature was the equivalent of being able to turn off bad radio stations to a pleasant song of my choosing, at any time and without any annoying commercials.

Getting out of bed was somewhat effortless, as well. Sure, my body wasn't 16 years old anymore and my legs were usually pretty tight; however, my body felt pretty good. As I showered, I felt the water sprays removing dirt and microbes from my body as if to also be cleansing my soul. After toweling off, I felt alive and vibrant like I was glistening. Glistening was certainly a new feeling for me and I liked it!

The normal drive wasn't too bad. My neck was flexible enough today to handle the rubbernecking. I think it was back in the same judo class that the Sensei asked us the question, "What is stronger? An oak tree or a reed? Most of the boys answered with a growl and a shot of testosterone, "The Oak!" they yelled. The girls countered with the same measure of estrogen and shouted, "The reed!" It seemed that their biochemistry made their selection for them and predisposed their answers, as well.

The Sensei, with a smile, knowing that a teaching moment was at hand, answered "It depends! If there was a strong, violent wind, the oak tree could fall down, where the reed could bend with the wind and still stay in the ground." This analogy reminded me to embrace my old Laura nature knowing it was temporary like the wind, and simply transform into my eternal Buddha nature.

"Hmm..." I planted another *mental flag* to ask the Buddha about time, impermanence and eternity!

The drive to work was much easier. I transformed my environment using **The Priceless Technique Number Two!** I saw the cars on the streets and freeway transforming into metallic lotus flowers carrying their Buddhas. I still chuckled to myself that this idea was pretty cool and hoped the Buddha would be proud of my innovation. The drive seemed much easier than normal. Instead of stops and starts, there seemed to be an ebb and flow that was far more pleasurable. My *Laura-self* tried to make my neck tighten and tried to suggest that nothing was pleasurable about rush hour traffic. She tried to dissuade me from thinking that the traffic was moving better. My *Buddha-self* allowed the voice to go way by calming me and reminding me that she was just an illusion. Besides, even if the traffic wasn't moving faster, *in reality* it didn't matter as I was relaxed, smiling, happy, and it was all an illusion anyway. So, I made it a good one and that was all that mattered!

I arrived at work earlier than normal. I was supposed to be at work at 7:30 AM, but arrived in the parking lot at 7:14. I normally made it to work at 7:28. Sally, the receptionist was smiling. I saw the office as a Buddha Field and immediately breathed a little calmer and slower. I greeted a few of my co-workers with a smile in the kitchen. Norma and Patricia paused with a discerning look and stared at me for a moment. I smiled a little more as I didn't understand their confusion.

Norma and Patricia looked at each other and then at me. And, in unison they asked "What is with you? What are you on?" I'd partied with both of them and always had a *good time*. Before I could get out a reply, Patricia leaned over and asked, "What are you taking? Do you have any extra?" I smiled now even bigger. They weren't used to seeing me be so happy, especially in the morning and especially without some mood-altering substance to change my perspective on life.

I started to explain the *Buddha-thing* and realized that if I did, they'd probably really think I was high. I said, "I'm smiling because I'm happy! Now Norma got closer and said, "Girl, who'd you hook up with last night?" I laughed again. I remembered that the illusion was all based on perception. Sadly, I realized that in their perceptions of the world and of me, it required external stimulants in order to be happy. It was either a substance, or some stud.

I calmly again explained that I was happy and that I truly felt joy in my heart. I asked how they both were doing. Again, they paused, and I realized that I normally wasn't asking people about their day, as I was more focused on me and my world. I was normally so self-centered, that I didn't care about theirs.

I quickly deployed **Priceless Technique Number Three** and saw my co-workers as Buddhas. It seemed to take a few seconds but by mentally blessing them, they too started to smile. Now I couldn't get either of them to shut up, as they were so happy. They were both excitedly telling me about their adventures from the night before. I chuckled inside. Being a Buddha certainly reduced my stress and was kind of fun!

We returned to our respective desks and cubicles. I turned on my dialer and quickly immersed myself in engaging conversations.

Weekend at Bennie's

It was now Friday morning and since the review with the Buddha on Tuesday, I'd had a pretty great week! I had slept well, got along with my sister and hadn't partied every night. Instead, I spent time at home and watched a couple of good movies. I did a little research on Meetup.com, and found a good meditation group; thinking this might help me even more with my new way of thinking. I found one that was rated the best in the area and put it on my calendar for next week. My daily commuting had been pretty calm. My new sales campaign was going well, and I was feeling great in my new custom-tailored *Buddha-Suit.*

The office was abuzz with the prospect of the festivities at hand over Memorial Day weekend. My friend Bennie was having his annual, big Memorial Day weekend party. We affectionately dubbed it *Weekend at Bennie's* and I was looking forward to attending it. In years past, this was one of my favorite weekends of the year.

For a moment, I realized the word *weekend,* if heard the wrong way sounded like *weakened.* Could it be that working all week made us weak and we needed time to recuperate? Or, if we partied too hard was that also the cause of being weakened?

Bennie's parents died in a drunk driving accident about four years ago. In addition to the Three Million Dollar Life Insurance Settlement, he also inherited the family's 14 Kentucky Fried Chicken stores, two houses, one near the beach, and the other on the lake which was only 90-minutes away. The weekend at Bennie's had many similarities to the movie. There was a house on the water and lots of partying. Bennie might have had worries in life, but worrying about money was not one of them. I'm guessing his biggest worry was whether people really liked him for him, or for his parties and money. Or, whether the long line of girls really liked him, or his endless supply of *stuff to* party with.

Being that it was a three-day weekend, our office closed at 1PM. I was going to meet Dena and Sandy at Dena's place, and we would drive to the lake house. I hadn't seen Dena all week since her visit to the hospital. And, I hadn't seen Sandy since she ditched us both at the hospital. While I like hanging out with Dena, Sandy was pretty bitchy most of the time and I wished she wasn't going with us to Bennie's.

The half-day at work went pretty well and pretty fast as most people I spoke with, were for the most part very friendly; making the hours go by even faster. After work, I went home to pack, say goodbye to my mom and luckily for me, missed my sister who was working. My mom and I had been getting along great, as we did most of the time. I never let her know how much partying I did, never wanting to worry or hurt her. Now in the car, I started thinking to myself "How was I going to handle this weekend?" If there was a grading system to being a Buddha for the week, then I'm sure I had a solid B. Maybe, a B minus at times… So, I thought that was pretty good! From fighting *Biker Barbie* to being a *Buddha B student* was not too bad! The Buddha was the best teacher I had ever had, and was happy that I was matching his efforts by being a good pupil.

I remembered back to the 70's TV Show *Kung Fu* where Cain, the student, was tested to see if he could remove a pebble from the Master's hand. I wondered if I was ready to *Take the Pebble from my Master's Hand?!* I quickly realized the Buddha wasn't teaching me to physically fight, he was teaching me to fight my inner demons. While the test of taking a pebble from a teacher's hand looked pretty difficult, not taking a beer from a friendly hand, or a bag of *stuff* from a pusher's hand was even tougher. These would be my *tests*...

I was going to be staying in Bennie's guest house, which could accommodate 10 people. The weekend and the group of people would offer many *tests,* as there would be many temptations. I realized my dreams of *taking the pebble* might be a little premature. I was more likely to be walking around with a pebble in my shoe.

As I started thinking about failing my *tests* it felt like my Buddha-Suit was starting to fray...

The first problem at hand was getting through the commute. The normal 90-minute drive was going to easily be two and a half hours with all the other drivers trying to get out of town, as well. Underneath my *Buddha-Suit,* which was **Priceless Technique Number One,** I wore a ruffled pair of shorts with a buttoned down top and bikini bra. When I drove down the freeway ramp the pace was already pretty slow. Oh my, there was a lot of traffic. I tried to deploy **Technique Number Two** and saw the cars as metallic lotus flowers.

Dena was in the front seat. She had on a similar outfit to mine, but her body was a little more protruding than mine. Her *girls* were certainly peeking out between the buttons of her blouse, and *ready to party.* This was typical Dena, as she was always the life of the party, and was always vying for attention. And, attention she got!

Sandy was in the backseat, and pulled a flask out of her backpack asking if we wanted a swig. While this was normal behavior in the past, I now felt more aware and was uncomfortable with her behavior. I suddenly cared that since I was driving, it would be me who was charged with an *Open Container* if we were pulled over by the *Popo.* Or, more accurately a *Chip* since we were on a California highway.

Trying to be more *Buddha-like,* my normally rough and direct speech had become softer. I had noticed that when speaking softer, people seemed to like me more, but my words didn't seem to have the same power. This hypothesis was proven when I asked Sandy to throw the flask in the trunk. She went off on a tangent and said, "What the fuck, Laura?" She continued, "Why? What's got your panties in an uproar? It's just Jack with a splash of Coke and if you don't want it, I'll just drink it all myself."

I again, trying to be *Buddha-like,* explained that it wasn't whether I liked it or not; it was the law, and I'd be the one who'd get prosecuted if we were pulled over. We argued a couple minutes before she finally mumbled, "What a bitch!" under her breath, took one last gulp before tightening the flask, then shoved the bottle in between the openings in the back seat.

I was pretty proud of myself for this one minor victory. While it was only minor, it was my first and that was major. This weekend was going to be a series of bouts where hopefully, I'd emerge as the champ. Dena then got a call from Elizabeth, who was already at the house with a few of her friends. The house was going to be full of people who were invited to stay and probably a long list of people who weren't invited but were staying anyway.

After three and half hours of driving, we were finally about fifteen minutes away from being at the house which was just outside of Barstow on a private lake called, Lake Jody. It wasn't a huge lake, but the area was big enough for riding on all of Bennie's Toys; which consisted of boating, waterskiing, jet skiing, motorcycles, and for one or more lucky girls, Bennie. The lake was private, and only to be used for the thirty or so homes that were lakefront. Most people driving on the main street probably didn't even know it existed unless you knew the name of the two inconspicuous streets that gained entry to this mini-island paradise.

When we drove up, the party was already in full force and it was only 5PM! We missed the traditional *4:20* round of shots and bong hits. Then it hit me… *4:20PM* used to be one of my favorite times in the day. My solar plexus started growling, the demons inside wanted to break free of their cage. Would I have the willpower to keep my demons at bay, and end my addictions? And, did I really even want to? What would my friends say?

The tunes were jamming on the outside speakers, and the group was gathered around the volleyball court. Again, no expense was spared for the *Weekend at Bennie's!* Bennie always had a thing for Dena. Bennie and I spent some time in detention together in Junior high, and I was the one who introduced him to Dena. We got together a time or two, but that was back in ninth grade and he had clearly moved on. I was one of the first people to call him when his parents died, and I think that meant a lot to him. I guess he thought of me as one of his real friends. Judging by the group, everyone was vying for a position as Bennie's *entourage*. Bennie didn't have movie star looks but was good looking enough for maybe a commercial, or two, and was my version of *Vinnie Chase*.

We were quickly welcomed and even before we grabbed our bags out of the car, Dena and Sandy were chugging beers out of the standard party-fair red solo cups. Bill Landers tried to give me one and I said "No, not right now..." He said, "What! This is a party and I needed to leave all that work shit behind! Joe, grab her a shot too!" We drank *Jello-shots* and they were *wwwiiickkkeeeddd!* I realized my *Buddha-Suit* was now developing holes... "How was I going to deal with the inner demons of my addictions and the peer pressure of my friends?" Reflexively, I grabbed the beer and took a few swigs to allow some of the steam of the peer pressure to release.

With the drink in my left hand, I grabbed one of my bags to prevent someone from putting something in my right, and moved toward the guest house. Once I was through the front door, I went to our room, put my stuff on my bed and sat down. My heart was racing... my *Buddha-Suit* was now coming apart at the seams. I remembered the Buddha and all the time he invested in me; guilt if used properly could be a powerful motivator. I was trying to use this guilt for good.

I closed my eyes and reaffirmed I was a Buddha. I sat there in silence for just under a minute, and I could feel the stitching on my *Buddha-jacket* starting to regain its form. As if this was happening by Angels, or what I think the Buddhist's called *Dakinis;* the wrinkles were being straightened and ironed out. The holes were being energetically sewn together. The taste of beer tasted good, but my inner *Laura-voice* pushing me to drink more, was gone. "Maybe some of the demons had left," I wondered.

Dena walked in and asked me if I was okay. Not wanting to get into the details of what I was truly experiencing, I said, "Yes! Let's go have some fun!" We both checked ourselves out in the bathroom, applied some extra touches to our makeup and made our way outside.

We had about two hours left of sunshine and jumped into the volleyball game. A little Def Leppard *Pour Some Sugar on Me* was blasting from the outdoor speakers. We were dancing, probably more than playing volleyball. Each time the ball was hit out of bounds it gave us time for dancing and singing along with the lyrics. To keep from being offered more alcohol, I nursed my beer. I was way below my average. Dena and Sandy were midway through their third beer and had an additional shot or two.

As the sun was setting, several of us jumped in Bennie's boat and went for a leisurely paced *sunset cruise* around the lake. Lake Jody was small and at times could be quite peaceful. This time of day was one of them. Each house from what I could gather, were mostly handed down from generation to generation. It had a homey community feel to it. Bennie's boat had a decent sound system. When Heart's song *Alone* came on, I suddenly felt alone.

When I sang the moving and passionate lyrics to the beat of the music, I felt *alone,* when in fact, I was actually surrounded by lots of people. I realized I felt this way because I felt different from my friends. I didn't feel part of this group. However, I remember feeling part of the group when I was consuming alcohol and drugs. Suddenly, on some level, I understood that these substances gave me a connection. On one level, my emotions were sad because I felt separated. At the same time, I gained a new realization that I was able to think and feel, and these were different emotions altogether. I could feel sadness, and at the same time thinking with clarity generated comfort

To counter the sadness and amplify the comfort, I started re-applying the **Third Priceless Technique,** which was imagining people and surroundings as Buddhas and a Buddha Field. First, I rapidly saw myself as a Buddha. My sadness started waning and was being replaced by a sweet contentment ebbing over into joy. Second, I improvised from the *rush-hour-traffic* technique that I came up with earlier, and imagined the boat as a giant metallic lotus flower. All of us on the boat were transformed into Buddhas, and were floating on a lake in the heavens. Lastly, I then imagined the houses on the lake as if they were also floating in the sky. The people in the houses were then transformed into Buddhas emanating golden light. "Whoa!" I immediately felt the connection with others that I was seeking, and lacking only moments ago. This connection and high was even better than one from any substances. Everyone was singing along with the song, which certainly helped to create a vibe of harmony. This **Third Priceless Technique** elevated my experience to entirely new levels.

The compatibility of the group at this moment was sublime which reminded me of my cousin, who was a great baseball player in high school. After a game where he had three home runs, he later told us that his perception of the ball had slowed down. He said he could see the rotation and almost became one with the ball. Our boat ride, from my perception was like his baseball game - moving in slow motion. The singing, the swaying back in forth in tune, the gentle currents in the water, with all of us floating in an imaginary lotus flower - we were all in harmony. We were in a Buddha Field!

It was at this moment a speed boat came flying by with a big group of girls taking off their tops and our Buddha Field moment was diminished. I realized I hadn't mastered being a Buddha and hadn't been able to maintain that state with outside interruptions. The boys in our boat showed they weren't at all close to being Buddhas either, as they started howling at the girls. I was able to stay in my personal Buddha Field for a few seconds longer and gradually fell down into reality. Having only left the Buddha Field for a moment, I now yearned to go back. This moment in time was so pure and so much better than any high; I couldn't wait to experience it again. "Maybe, like using guilt in the proper way, I was going to use my addictive tendencies to motivate me to constantly be in a Buddha Field?" I rumored.

We started heading back, grabbed some dinner and eventually plopped down in chairs next to the fire pit. I was nursing another beer, as compared to maybe seven or so for Dena and Sandy. I was grateful that since our arrival, everyone was too busy with their own drinking and partying to be concerned about my lack of consumption.

Thunderstruck by AC/DC blared on. This song usually got people pretty pumped up. For some reason, a thought popped into my head to create a Buddha Field. Overcome by my usual *Laura-self,* I thought, "Yeah right, a Buddha Field sure wouldn't work with these people loudly singing *Thunderstruck!*" However, I wanted to give it a try. So this time I applied ALL **Three Priceless Techniques** with my eyes open and awareness to keep it going. Turn myself into a Buddha, check! Turn our fire pit area into a Buddha Field, check! I wasn't sure if this was ok or not, but I came up with an idea. I remembered one night I was flipping channels on TV and saw a bunch of monks performing a ceremony around a fire. I think they were somewhere near Tibet. I imagined we were Buddhas in Tibet doing a fire ceremony. Just these **Two Priceless Techniques** were changing me for sure! I could feel the outside stimulus of the pounding bass of the guitars and drums from Bennie's impressive sound system; it was almost like the Buddha Field around me shielded me from these chaotic, thunderous beats.

I progressed to seeing others as Buddhas, but then I started having a little difficulty with **Priceless Technique Number Three.** I questioned, why was I having such difficulty? It wasn't as if any of these people didn't like me, except for maybe Kay. Kay was kind of a bitch, but that wasn't it... I realized that a Buddha wouldn't call someone a bitch, and chuckled at my usual juvenile ways. I allowed myself to take a deep breath and relax. Since, a Buddha is omniscient and has all the answers, I was trying my best to tap into thought-pool of wisdom. I then sunk deeper in my Buddha Nature, and became clear on the root cause of the problem.

The problem was me and with my ego. Now that I learned the **Three Priceless Techniques,** I inaccurately saw myself as better than these people. I was in the process of overcoming my addictions, but was only slightly ahead of the group on the *Buddha Scale.* Now that I was judging them, I was magnifying all of these peoples' negative traits. I was labeling them as addicts and focusing on their dark energies around them; thus, I immediately felt my Buddha Nature disappearing, and the Buddha Field shrinking around the group. Needless to say, I was bummed. While the others were singing such a hardcore song by AC/DC, the **Techniques** were working until I failed in the application of **Priceless Technique Number Three.**

Failure! Wow, failure hurt! I remember the first time I felt like a failure when I was a young girl and disappointed my mom. I remember resolving that I never wanted to feel that pain and discouragement again. The sad part was, instead of using my pain as a motivation to succeed, I reversed this mental leverage to one of mental bondage. In trying to escape, I used substances, so I wouldn't have to feel; instead of dealing with the pain. I was now shackled to my addictions. While my substances provided me a temporary cessation from pain, it created a long-term bondage to something worse; addictions. Pain was bad enough, but being addicted *and* in pain, was worse!

This failure realization was a powerful one, and added it to my list of fears as one of the themes in my life, along with shame. Instead of further digging a deeper hole in self-suffering, or like the Buddha taught me, *Samsara;* I decided I wanted to change the reflexive response within me! Maybe the experiences of being a Buddha was still lingering in my consciousness as I was still tapping into the enlightenment that was within me. And that part felt good!

As the night dwindled, I was probably averaging about 50% on my *Buddha Meter* and thought that was better than OK. In fact, I felt great. I had only two beers and while I enjoyed the taste of beer, I didn't feel like I had to drink it, and certainly wasn't craving something harder. That was huge for me. "Could it be that I was no longer addicted?" This was so fast and so easy! I had already known that these teachings were powerful, but I was still coming to the realization that I was an actual Buddha. And, that I had the ability to not only transform my life and consciousness; but transform all those around me. This was the most powerful thing I had ever learned!

It was just before midnight and the crackling fire was gasping to stay alive. I, on the other hand, was still in awe of how alive I felt. Half of the group was already passed out, and the rest were just about to go to bed. As I walked to the guesthouse, I looked up at the bright moon in the sky. It was so big. For a moment I thought I saw a *rainbow aura* around it. We had heard on the radio on the drive up that it was a Full Moon and Lunar eclipse on Sunday night. I wondered if that was going to make things extra crazy over the weekend.

I took off my makeup, brushed my teeth and made it into bed. As I lied there, I mentally reviewed my day and graded myself at a B+. I hadn't had a B+ in school since around sixth grade so was feeling pretty good about it. Pleasantly, my mom came into mind, and I thought she would be proud of me, which made me smile more. I put on my *Buddha-Suit*; this suit was made of the finest wool and silk and I looked good! I saw the house we were in as a *Buddha Mansion* in the sky and even before I started seeing others as Buddhas, I was so blissed out that I mentally floated away. Time literally stopped, and I just melted into bliss.

Bennie, Boats and Booze!

With my eyes still closed, I could hear the birds singing with their morning greeting. It seemed they were giving it extra gusto to inspire us to wake up, get out of bed and join their celebration of the new day. I was feeling inspired. I was one of the first ones up. I made it to the bathroom first, brushed my teeth, washed my face and used the toilet.

The morning was beautiful! Seventy-two degrees and it was only 7:30 AM. I walked outside and watched the sun glisten across the lake. I watched some adorable birds, who were serenading us while sitting on the biggest tree on Bennie's lot. For the first time since I was a kid, I felt a connection to nature. It was at this moment I realized I hadn't put on my *Buddha-Suit* and thought I'd better apply the **Three Priceless Techniques** before my day got underway.

Already calm and very peaceful, which was very unlike me, I closed my eyes and imagined the Golden Buddha coming down into my body. I immediately got goose bumps and felt a surge of energy. I imagined myself as the Buddha and merged him into my heart and vice versa. Again, I felt even more goose bumps and even more energy. My calmness and peace levels continued climbing, and now I noticed joy burgeoning from my heart. I smiled from ear to ear! I continued by visualizing the area around me turning into a Buddha Field. Since there weren't any humans within eyeshot, I instead imagined the birds and all the people in the houses turning into Buddhas.

When I opened my eyes for a brief second, I was able to see *rainbow auras* around the birds. These rainbows seemed to be about two inches thick. I got excited seeing these auras, but I think my excitement dropped the auras from my visibility. I then remembered back to my high school physics class that the visible light spectrum was 380 to 700 *something,* and was only about three percent of the light spectrum. I couldn't remember what that *something* was called so I allowed myself to relax further into my enlightened Buddha Nature. I knew it wasn't inches or kilometers, but what was it? I now noticed a new pattern of *being.*

My normal pattern of *being* was barely noticing my outer environment which was probably due to my inner environment not being able to relax. I was always nervous and looking for something external to calm me. I looked at the lake as if it was a metaphor for my consciousness. When the waters were agitated and undulating up and down from the action of the boats and people, I was unable to see into the water and the depth below. I often had times of not remembering things which was probably due to the *agitated waters* of my emotions and thoughts. I closed my eyes again and tried to elevate my Buddha self. In doing so, I felt very calm and could feel the calmness of the environment around me, which I again saw as a Buddha Field. Aha! I remembered the term used to measure light was called *Nano-meters.* My teacher, Mr. Kirsch, used to joke that light was faster than sound and his students looked bright until they spoke. Back then, I didn't find his sarcastic humor funny, but I chuckled now. He was so right. I guess it was like *Doppler humor.* I had seen it before I actually *heard* it, as it took years to sink in.

I further made an important realization. I suddenly realized that the brighter my aura, the brighter I'd be! I contemplated this deeper. I now understood that partaking in substances that altered my consciousness would make my aura dark. This would not only keep me in the illusion of suffering; it would dumb me down. Whoa! The Buddha was really rubbing off on me… I think he'd be proud of my revelations. The more *stuff* I took, the more I concentrated on dramas and traumas. I remembered this was the same with Sandy. Wherever Sandy went, drama was sure to follow. She usually pushed the limits of her addictions, and *her* dramas also got *us* sucked into some pretty serious traumas.

I remembered one night where some guys wanted to take us back to their place. Sandy denied their advances so one of the guys pulled a knife to her throat accusing her of teasing them too much, and that she should be punished for it. I realized as I was thinking about this, I started feeling heavier. I could feel the *etheric dirt* on my aura. Whoa! It was heavy! I guess the reality of this memory was heavy, and was quite scary; so, it would make sense the energy would be heavy too. I felt like I needed a shower after thinking about this altercation. I thought I'd imagine myself standing under a waterfall being cleansed by the drops of water. It took maybe a minute or so using this visualization and suddenly I felt quite a bit cleaner and lighter!

I had so much positive energy from applying the *3PT's*, as I now nicknamed them; that I decided to do something positive and productive with this energy. Normally, when I felt *energized,* it was really frenetic like an ungrounded wire bouncing energy everywhere. This frenetic energy usually got me into trouble. This new energy felt strong and stable, and more importantly grounded. I decided to go inside and start making breakfast for everyone.

Only half of the group was up. With half still sleeping and the other half getting ready, I was the first to make it into the kitchen. I fired up the coffee pot as I didn't think the Buddha would mind me having a little caffeine. I looked for the pancake mix, bowls, butter, and the eggs in the refrigerator.

The ingredients were all gathered. One of the guys, Ted, came down the hall from one of the bedrooms near Bennie's big room. He lively greeted me with "Good morning! What are you doing?" I could tell he didn't mean it in a sarcastic way. He was genuinely surprised that I'd be doing this and also seemed quite pleased.

I replied with "Good morning Ted" and poured him a cup of java. He smiled, said it was mighty kind of me and drank a few sips. He grabbed a seat at the kitchen bar area which allowed me to look at his well-formed pecs and stomach. Yes, Ted had his shirt off, which made this morning go even better. We were making small talk while I was cracking the eggs and mixing up the pancake mix. I realized that while I visualized all the people in the houses around Lake Jody as Buddhas earlier this morning, I hadn't specifically imagined him as a Buddha.

So, I then imagined him as a Buddha. "Whoa!" the energy was incredible. While physically I was attracted to his pecs, abs, and happy demeanor; now I felt something different. It was like we merged. "Wow!" abruptly went off in my head. I could feel the connection, as if I was channeling my high school Physics teacher and realized the word connection was actually *connect ions*. How appropriate, because I had my eyes on Ted and we were definitely connecting. I chuckled inside...

At this moment Sandy walked in and the connectivity between Ted and I dropped. She busted out, "Let's get this party started!" and continued making a lot of noise all while looking for the Bloody Mary Mix. She found it right away, and condescendingly asked me where the celery was located. Before I could get a word out, she had already found it and quickly started making the drinks. She was a like a whirlwind, or more like a tornado - making a lot of sound and moving around violently in the kitchen. If she were a kitchen appliance she'd surely be a blender. As she added the mix and the vodka in the blender, the ice cubes were crackling loudly like an alarm calling all the party-goers to the kitchen. The ice crashing into the spinning blade was every bit like the smell of a bitch in heat to a pack of wild dogs. Just about everyone was now up, eleven total, with six girls and five guys. My beautiful Buddha Field was evaporating like ice cubes on the 4th of July. Unfortunately, my connection with Ted was also going away. This was the first connection I felt with another guy in a very long time.

While Sandy was getting plenty of attention sharing her concoction, I was quietly plating a pancake or two, and some scrambled eggs onto paper plates. As I was placing the plates in front of people, I was getting a mixture of reactions. Some acknowledged me with a very sincere smile, saying "Thanks!" and some were more sarcastic asking, "What got into you?" This morphed into "Who got into to you?" and still evolved into "Who are you?" along with variations of these themes. No matter their response, I just humbly smiled and realized how good it felt serving others.

Music was playing from the big speakers next to the TV. The lyrics "Jukebox Hero, he's got stars in his eyes..." was playing and suddenly these words had more meaning to me. I could feel a different energy from the *"stars in their eyes."* Each person looking at me had a different energetic signature. It was as if their eyes had laser beams and were pointing at me. The grateful people were like a diffused laser that sent out soft, fluffy light making me feel good which magnified my happiness. The "ungrateful thanks!" comments without much connection, had little effect on me. The sarcastic ones were, imagining what it looked like from the *Buddha Balcony*, consisting of a red laser that was prickly and prodding me with heat in the face and heart. They were like the jabs of a boxer testing his target and deciding when, or if, to apply a *knockout blow.* I made a conscious effort to let these punches go too! I also realized that prior to meeting the Buddha, I was walking around the world and reacting negatively due to the stimuli that was coming at me, or what I had consumed.

So, I resolved that these *prickly jabs* were not going to have much effect on me, especially since I felt more like a Buddha. And, more importantly, I didn't need to put up my gloves, defend my face, shield my body, or deliver a counterpunch. The more I was in my *Buddha-Suit,* the more I had a *Buddha-Shield* around me, and to a degree was immune to their attacks.

Speaking of attacks, Sandy, who had already had a couple drinks in her, tried to give me a Bloody Mary, but I politely declined. She looked at me with those *red lasers.* She definitely sent this out as a *jab* and was deciding on whether she should go for the knockout punch. I slipped the jab like a boxer, countered with a smile and said, "Let me clean up the dishes first." I knew with just a little time, her attention would be somewhere else, and she'd undoubtedly forget about my drinking participation, or lack thereof. Instead she diverted with a sarcastic remark of "Breakfast and now dishes? Did you get laid last night? What got into you?" The group, of course laughed and were quickly re-directed by Bennie saying, "Let's go for a ride on the boat!"

Bennie put his arm around my shoulders and offered me first up for skiing, since I made breakfast for everyone. I smiled and politely declined, backing up my earlier statement that I needed to do the dishes. He said genuinely, "OK, are you sure? It's hard to deny a beautiful lady wanting to do dishes."

I also hadn't been called a "beautiful lady" in a long time. There was a time that I longed for words like that; however, with my *Buddha-Suit,* while he meant them as a compliment, the words seemed so hollow and meaningless. I realized how people's looks could further trap them into *Samsara* - both good and bad. If someone was perceived by others as good looking, they were a magnet for wanted and unwanted affection. If a person was say, unattractive, they might be left longing for affection, and thus a disconnect with others. I was really treasuring all of these new realizations. "Thank you, Buddha,!" I said with a brief head turn upward.

I smiled for a second, as I remembered the scene from the movie, *Limitless* where Bradley Cooper was in the hallway of his apartment complex and the brain enhancement drug had kicked-in. He was able to read a girl down the halls' book at a distance and was able to advise her the crafting of her legal paper. I was also starting to feel like that. He called it a *sparkling cocktail of useful information* in the movie. My brain's thoughts were the clearest they had ever been. My senses were also heightened. The best part is this state of being was *legal,* had access to an unlimited supply, and there wouldn't be a crash.

Bennie grabbed the boat keys off the wall, looked my way and said, "Last chance?!" I smiled again and said "Thanks, go have fun!" Two guys and three girls including Sandy and Dena ran out too. Just about everyone went outside except for Ted, who volunteered to help me dry the dishes as I washed them. I greatly accepted Ted's offer to stay. While I hadn't mentally recreated the *Kitchen Buddha Field,* it seemed to magically recreate itself. From this I learned that while others might not be aware of a Buddha Field, to a degree they can sure help in the creation!

We had great conversation and were really re-connecting. We finished the dishes in about ten minutes. I poured us each another cup of coffee as we went outside. We sat down on the deck with our feet dangling in the water. We watched the Boats and WaveRunners whoosh by. The lake was very crowded due to the Holiday. Bennie was a smart guy and always liked to go a few laps around the lake before he would pull the first skier of the day.

A muscular kid probably around nineteen years of age was on a Waverunner and riding pretty close to the boat. Both Ted and I were conversing and loosely watching the Lake scene while gazing into each other's eyes. The Lake wasn't that big so you could easily hear people laughing and talking from all sides. Suddenly, Sandy and Dena stood up, pulled off their bikini tops and were whistling to get the boy's attention.

The first rule of riding on a Waverunner is you need to throttle the gas button to make a turn. This rule is critical because when the throttle button is pushed, the jet is able to propel the craft through the turns. It's quite common for new riders when scared, to let go of the throttle making the Waverunner continue on its current trajectory. The girls sure got the boys' attention. The boy turned towards the boat and yelled, "How do I stop?!" Just then, replaced by a loud crashing sound, his watercraft crashed into the side of Bennie's boat.

Dena went flying head first into the water, ejecting over the boy's head. The boat's frame from our perspective, looked to be severely damaged. Jim, one of the guys on the boat, dove into the water after Dena - she was not floating. Lake Jody was a small private lake so wearing life jackets, while it was the law, was more of a suggestion here. The boat was vastly taking on water. Mike grabbed his cell and called 911. A few boats that were distributed throughout the lake were now headed towards our group. Jim quickly emerged out of the water with Dena towing her by her shoulders to one of the other boats. A muscular guy from that boat pulled them up onto the deck and appeared to lay her down. It was hard to see everything from our perspective, but he had the physicality of a policeman or fireman and was probably giving CPR.

Bennie's boat was gradually sinking. The rest of our group were now on the other boats, with all eyes on Bennie's boat, except for Bennie and another guy who were trying to tie a rope to the bow of the boat. It looked as if they were successful as they yelled what appeared to be instructions back and forth between them and the *towboat*. The muscular guy who was working on Dena stood up and yelled. "She is awake!" There were yells of "Oh my god!" "Thank you!" "Great job!", and alike.

The sirens from the paramedics and firemen were heard at a distance, and soon were rolling into Bennie's gated compound. While the medics and crew were getting stretchers and other lifesaving tools, others were going to the dock to survey for fire. The boat Dena was on was the first to make it to the dock, followed by the boat with the poor kid who crashed. He was bleeding pretty badly along with some pretty deep wounds. A couple more boats came in and dropped off the rest of our group followed by a boat towing Bennie's vessel.

Dena was on a stretcher and placed in an ambulance. They took her to a local hospital. The boy was being examined, and a couple of his friends showed up to support him. Evidently, the kid wasn't injured too badly. The paramedics examined the rest of our group. Sandy had a broken finger and a laceration on her face. The rest were a little bruised and mostly just shaken up.

The rest of the day was pretty surreal. It was interesting that I was using the word *surreal* to describe the *real* world, as it was also turning into a *real-time montage*. The group went to the hospital. However, Bennie and one of his friends stayed behind to tend to his boat. We had to wait a while before a doctor came out. Eventually, the doctor explained that Dena suffered some injuries upon impact. These injuries included a concussion, some cuts and a broken femur. The boy had just a few cuts. Sandy, being her drama queen self, had to get in on the action too. She had a broken finger and needed some stitches on her face.

Moments later, we greeted Dena in her room. Sandy was there, and, per usual, was complaining up a storm. Bennie and his friend, later arrived at the hospital and updated us on the condition of the boat. It had a gaping hole, but was saved. After several hours at the hospital, Dena was finally released. We all caravanned back to Bennie's place.

While Sandy was the last one in the front door, she was the first one at the bar. She grabbed a bottle of her good friend *Jose Cuervo Tequila.* She wanted something *to kill the pain.* She said, "This shit will to-kill ya!" One of the guys grabbed a shot with her and they started pouring one for everyone. The group was pretty stressed and wanted to blow off some steam. Two guys went outside and lit a bong as they were talking about needing to take the edge off. Sandy offered me a shot. I took it and gave her a little smile and a head nod.

It was at this moment that the montage stopped. While we were in *real-time,* I realized how unconscious I lived my life. I spent the hours after the crash on autopilot. I was like the young kid, who forgot the first rule of riding a WaveRunner - you need to use the throttle to steer. I had not applied the **First Priceless Technique**, as this was important to *steer* my life in the right direction. I was ensnared by *Samsara's clutches.* I was her personal bitch.

I took a deep breath to fill my brain with much needed oxygen. I also craved the energy that was fueled by my deep breathing. At that moment in time, I decided enough was enough. I was no longer *Samsara's Bitch.* I was a Buddha!

Buddha to BE!

The world of *Samsara* was certainly spinning around and around at Bennie's place. Dena was on the couch, and a little doped up on pain medication. Sandy was self-medicating with *Jose*. Some of the guys were toking it up outside while the rest were drinking, and again, I was the lone sober one.

I decided to put on my *Buddha-Suit*. I unanticipatedly realized that calling it a *Buddha-Suit* was disrespectful. I also thought that it also implied an impermanence. A more correct name would be *Buddha-Skin* since I wear the same skin every day. Though, *Buddha-Skin* still didn't sound appropriate either, and also seemed kind of tacky. On the other hand, skin was also impermanent, as one day I would be beyond having this body and would be a Buddha!

I was committed to becoming a Buddha and cultivating my Buddha Nature. Once again, I began to envision the Golden Buddha coming down as we merged into each other's heart center. The *languaging* of *Buddha-Suit* or *Buddha-Skin* was long gone. The words that came to me, were just *BEing!* This distinction was powerful! I could feel that I owned this Buddha Nature at a whole new level. It was almost like a video game where my accomplishments and victories earned new levels and received promotions like Sergeant, Major or Colonel. I was becoming a Buddha! And that was far greater than any man-made title.

I started seeing myself as a Buddha. With that imagery, my energy was radiating outward. I could feel its radius expanding. It was time to deploy the **Second Priceless Technique**, and see the room and the area around Lake Jody as a Buddha Field.

I again, was making new breakthroughs in my consciousness. I realized that while it was great to be a Buddha, that wasn't enough. I felt a hint of sadness and compassion. By being a Buddha, I now felt an empathy for others, and wanted others to become Buddha as well. I could feel this new awareness and enthusiasm deep within my being. I saw the world as *real* and saw the Buddha as *realer* with my new set of eyes. I now visualized my friends through a more compassionate filter, as they were stuck, like I once was, in *Samsara.* I laughed inside as I jokingly said, "I need to help these bitches..." While half joking and with a smile, I imagined them as Buddhas. In my mind they were glowing, dispersing the darkness of *Samsara* and saw them elevating themselves into a bright light. Their bodies were still here, but their energy bodies were glowing with a resurgence. They lit up the area around Lake Jody. My friends were no longer *adult elephants* shackled to inconsequential stakes in the ground.

I was also radiating energy and all of our collective energies were merging! Bennie's place was now a *Buddha Palace*. White light was glowing everywhere. Whoa! I could feel the waves of pulsating vibration. If we were listening to a song, it would have been called *HeavenStruck!* Each person was energetic and seemed to look younger and healthier. The guys who were lighting up outside came in the house, as they said they felt like they just needed to come inside.

We were standing around, and as amazing it sounds from the crazy *Samsara* filled day that we had, we were now, for the first time since we arrived, quite relaxed. Even Sandy who usually wore a scowl on her hardened features, was sort of smiling. A couple seconds later, the ground started shaking. It was Southern California after all, and we were having an earthquake. We looked at one another, grabbed the furniture and held on. Three waves rippled through the house and dissipated off into the distance.

Instead of freaking out, the group just rode the waves like surfers effortlessly navigating nature's raw power. For a moment, I laughed internally as this whole experience was so *surreal* and was as if I were *tripping*. While there was a little nervousness about our group, it was only about a 2.2 on a 10-magnitude scale of nervousness. The earthquake, on the other hand, was probably a 5.7 on the Richter scale judging by the dogs barking and car alarms going off in the distance. Had it not been for my self-created Buddha Field, we probably would have been about a 7+ on the nervousness scale. Who knows, maybe we were even able to minimize the earthquake's scale, as well!?

We quietly started hugging one another. We exchanged hugging partners and were sharing moments of connection looking into each other's eyes. Even Sandy was hugging and enjoying it. Dena used her crutches to get off the couch, and was also getting in on the hugging action. Again, this whole experience was so *surreal* and real at the same time. The room was filled with a visceral feeling of peace, connectedness and gratitude which was so unlike this group.

We all felt so intertwined and close. I had heard about *Tantric Yoga* and planted a *mental flag* to ask the Buddha what that was all about. I laughed inside as I recalled one of my favorite characters, Ari Gold, from the HBO show *Entourage.* We were paying homage to him as we were *hugging it out bitches!*

The hugging turned into appreciation for each other and words were shared like "I'm so glad you are OK!" "I don't know what I'd do without you!" "Thank you!" and the like. This *Kumbaya moment* had reached a crescendo. It was time for us go to our respective beds. To my astonishment, we ended with a group hug!

From Bitches to Buddhas Review

Now in my bed, my body was certainly ready for the restorative process known as sleep. My emotions under normal circumstances, would have been frazzled. The *old Laura* would have taken something to mask her fear from another earthquake. My mind and vision were clear and was grateful for all that I had learned today. I was marinating in this gratitude and fell asleep.

However long it was, I didn't know, nor did it matter. The glowing, golden light was approaching from a distance and the Buddha softly landed floating in front of me. He was floating on a giant white lotus flower, as if it was his personal *flying carpet.* He sat above me with a big smile.

I chuckled. Since the last time I saw him, he made an entrance with, "How was your day?" I wondered what he'd start up with for this conversation. He asked, "Bitches to Buddha, huh?!" He ended the sentence with his voice rising at the end, as if to say, "I give you pearls of wisdom and you make fake jewelry out of them." He smiled and said I did an excellent job! He reminded me that people only see the world through the perception of their consciousness, and what was taught of them. He complimented me stating I was doing the best I could with the whole *Buddha-Suit thing.* He also said a good teacher knows there are times to correct a student, and there are times where the student needs to learn for themselves.

He further went on to say that I was not only doing a good job, but I was learning and *earning* new levels, as was indicative of seeing these higher levels from the banal to the *Buddhic Realms.* I was evolving, but this required time, processing and even mistakes. He said, "There are only two mistakes one can make along the road to truth. Not going all the way and not starting."

He pushed the hilarious pause button as I processed the statement he had just made. I remembered that earlier in the day I had resolved not to be *Samsara's Bitch,* and that I was now on a *Buddha-Adventure* for truth. "I must go all the way!" I resolutely said in my mind.

The Buddha explained that we would review my day, as well as my progress, at a later date. He made it clear that it all needed to be reviewed in divine timing. For now, it was time for me to go on my *Buddha-Adventure.* I had a map, **The Three**

Priceless Techniques, which would steer me in the right direction. This was a process to earn and learn. Through practice, I would perfect my Buddha Nature. With that, he was gone!

The Buddha Fields Challenge

Thank you for reading *Buddha Fields for Addictions!* We hope you enjoyed the story!

Are you up for a challenge? While you might have trepidation about applying **The Three Priceless Techniques** as to whether they will work for you; we challenge you to take the **Buddha Fields Challenge!**

It is said that it takes twenty-one days to create a habit. The **Buddha Fields Challenge** is a commitment to practice **The Three Priceless Techniques** for the next twenty-one days. Put them to the test and see how you feel, how much you've progressed on your own *Buddha-Scale* and how much your world has improved!

It is also a good idea to read this book, at least once a week during this time, as you'll most assuredly gleam more and have more profound experiences.

As you read, the goal is to inspire seven million people to do **The Three Priceless Techniques** consistently. Please let us know that you are committed to this challenge and email us at BuddhaFieldsChallenge@gmail.com. We are here to support you in creating Global Buddha Fields Meditation Groups.

To further help you to improve your world and the world at large, we highly recommend you do the *Buddha Fields Blessing Meditation* daily. This twenty-two-minute meditation will accelerate your Buddha Nature and help the world to do the same. It is available to download at www.BuddhaFields.org for only $9.

Again, thank you for reading this book. We believe that a picture is worth a thousand words, and an experience is worth a million. While you may want to *tell* others about what you learned, it is better that you *recommend* the book to others; so they may have their own *experience*.

May we I you in the Buddha Fields!

Love and Tujechey, (Tibetan for, *May you achieve enlightenment in this incarnation*)

Daniel O'Hara

Acknowledgements

In my first book, *Buddha Fields,* this medium provided an opportunity to thank people in many areas of my life.

In this book I'd like to thank you, the **Buddha Green Tara** whom I was praying to about a job scenario and received the vision for the *Buddha Fields* books.

I'd also like to thank my main Spiritual Teacher **Maha Atma (Great Soul) Choa Kok Sui,** who for the last twenty-years has been the most amazing Spiritual Teacher, Mentor, like a Father, and Friend. He has shared with me so much and cared deeply for my family.

I'd also like to thank **His Eminence Tsem Tulku Rinpoche** and Pastor Seng Piow Loh for sharing the Holy Dharma with me. Their constant work for the benefit of all beings and modern communication of the Dharma will benefit all.

While this story might seem like a very, Non-Buddhist, Buddhist book, I take responsibility for any errors. It is my intention that the way the book was constructed is to lead others out of their suffering.

I'd like to the person, who would like to remain anonymous, you are an amazing lady! You have inspired many in our www.OCMeditationGroup.com to help others. Your story in overcoming addictions has been remarkable! And, your dedication to feeding, clothing and empowering the homeless, weekly for years has been AMAZING! Thank you for allowing *creative license* to be taken in the telling of your story. In much the same way a Hollywood film takes *Based on a True Story* - we did the same with Laura to make the sharing of **The Three Priceless Techniques** relatable.

When I write, I see the scenes in pictures and my fingers rapidly attempt to put them into print. This process can be a nightmare for an editor… (And, for me as well, as I see the scene in my mind and to maintain this flow, I think I have it flawlessly typed and that is far from the truth…)

I'd like to thank Eden O'Hara, who has spent many hours on the editing and helping to make key concepts more explainable. Her work has been vital!

Ms. Brenda Beza, whose several hundred edits took the book to more readable heights, thank you!

Helping with some key distinctions and editing, Laura Gatlin has helped the book greatly, despite her busy schedule!

Thank you Parie Petty of www.WesternLithographics.com for your amazing cover. You are so talented and I pray that more authors and businesses see your talent and hire you for their books, media and printing needs.

Lastly, I'd like to thank the OC Meditation Group, whom I have the honor to serve and for providing me much inspiration.

- Daniel O'Hara

About The Author

Daniel O'Hara has lived a unique life, marching to the beat of his own internal drummer. Identifying more with the philosophy of the East, he developed a love of the martial arts at an early age. While searching for martial arts instructors, he realized there was much more to be learned. He then sought out the mystical teachings of the East and found Maha Atma (Great Soul) Choa Kok Sui.

In 1987, at the young age of 19, he left UC Riverside and became a stockbroker. This was during the greed and glory days of Wall Street. He might have been the youngest stockbroker in Dean Witter's illustrious history. He experienced much pain, stress and some success. He became an expert in trading the commodity markets using the vibration of the planets and sacred geometry. This esoteric understanding of how vibration (energy) influences people, further pushed him to understand energy healing.

He has launched three book series- *Buddha Fields, Christ's Castle and Krishna's Kingdom.* He has helped bring five companies public and even completed a billion-dollar transaction. He has experienced the highest of highs and the lowest of lows in the world of finance.

After five years in the industry and only in his mid-twenties, he fell apart from stress and looked to rebuild his physical, mental and emotional life. Little did he know at the time that these life lessons would send him on a quest to develop spiritually.

Finding the priceless teachings of Maha Atma Choa, the Modern Founder of Pranic Healing, Daniel was given the tools of self-development, sharing profound wisdom, and healing others. Daniel has taught healing seminars in nine states and healed famous professional athletes from the NFL, NBA, MLB and UFC.

Daniel runs the www.OCMeditationGroup.com in Orange County, CA. He is very passionate about many causes including feeding/clothing the impoverished, working for animal rights, promoting sustainability issues and protecting the environment. He is also the co-founder of www.HealthePacificOcean.org, a portal to inspire people to meditate, daily blessing the challenges facing the Pacific Ocean.

Please become part of our Buddha Fields community, so we can stay in touch. https://www.facebook.com/BuddhaFields

For more information about Daniel, his meditations and video seminars, please see www.DanielOHara.com, www.Buddhafields.org and www.BuddhaParables.com.

www.ingramcontent.com/pod-product-compliance
Lightning Source LLC
Chambersburg PA
CBHW070936130626
46555CB00001B/451

* 9 7 8 0 9 9 7 8 8 1 8 2 0 *